C01 035 620X

D0807667

THE ISLAND THAT DIDN'T EXIST

OXFORD
UNIVERSITY PRESS

Great Clarendon Street, Oxford OX2 6DP
Oxford University Press is a department of the University of Oxford.
It furthers the University's objective of excellence in research, scholarship,
and education by publishing worldwide. Oxford is a registered trade mark
of Oxford University Press in the UK and in certain other countries

Copyright © Joe Wilson 2020
Illustration © George Ermos 2020

The moral rights of the author have been asserted

Database right Oxford University Press (maker)

First published 2020

All rights reserved. No part of this publication may be reproduced,
stored in a retrieval system, or transmitted, in any form or by any means,
without the prior permission in writing of Oxford University Press,
or as expressly permitted by law, or under terms agreed with the appropriate
reprographics rights organization. Enquiries concerning reproduction
outside the scope of the above should be sent to the Rights Department,
Oxford University Press, at the address above

You must not circulate this book in any other binding or cover
and you must impose this same condition on any acquirer

British Library Cataloguing in Publication Data

Data available

ISBN: 978-0-19-277509-2

1 3 5 7 9 10 8 6 4 2

Printed in India

Paper used in the production of this book is a natural,
recyclable product made from wood grown in
sustainable forests.The manufacturing process
conforms to the environmental regulations
of the country of origin.

DUNDEE CITY
COUNCIL

LOCATION
CENTRAL CHILDREN'S

ACCESSION NUMBER
COI 035 620 X

SUPPLIER   PRICE
ASK   £6.99

CLASS No.   DATE
                  31/3/21

THE ISLAND THAT DIDN'T EXIST

JOE WILSON

OXFORD
UNIVERSITY PRESS

Chapter 1

Rixon Webster was twelve years old and nothing in his world could surprise him.

He knew, for example, that when his mum's footsteps stopped outside his bedroom she wanted to talk. Even though his bedside clock flashed 23:17.

'Rixy, darling,' she said, opening the bedroom door. 'There's something I need to tell you.'

He grunted vaguely in reply. He thought about pretending to be asleep, but that never worked— his mum just perched on the bed until he stirred. In any case, Rixon had a 'responsibility' towards his mother now. That's what his dad said: a 'responsibility'.

So he fumbled for the bedside light and, as his eyes blinked open, he focused on his mum's expression.

She had made her lips all straight, and her eyebrows all low and frowny, so he knew what was coming. It was 'something serious'. In fact, if he wasn't mistaken, it was 'something sad'.

'Now, Rixon,' Mrs Webster began, 'I don't want you to be too upset.' Rixon sat up in bed, preparing to display just the right amount of upsetness. 'But I had a phone call just now, a very sad phone call,' his mum continued. 'There is just no easy way to say this, but I'm afraid I have to tell you . . . Uncle Silvester has died.'

This was the moment when Rixon was supposed to react, he knew that. There was just one problem: Rixon did not have the faintest idea who Uncle Silvester was. He thought he sounded a bit like a character from a play they'd done at school last summer. But it didn't seem right to mention that. So he just said nothing.

Luckily, it seemed as though that was just the right thing to do.

'Oh, darling. I can see how shocked you are.'

'Yes,' Rixon managed.

'I was the same,' his mum said. She was starting to bite her left thumbnail, which was a bad sign. She was getting anxious.

'So, when did you last see him?' Rixon asked hurriedly.

'Oh, see him, Silvester? Well, not for ages . . .' his mum admitted, 'but I loved him when I was a kid. He was so funny, so crazy, but kind. I suppose that's why I named you after him.'

Here was some news. After twelve years carrying the most ridiculous name in the school (if not the world) Rixon now had an explanation. Well, sort of.

'You just said he was called Uncle Silvester.'

'Yes.'

'Well, I'm not,' he said patiently.

'Oh no, that would have sounded silly. No, "Rixon" was his surname. He was my mother's brother, my uncle, your great-uncle, remember?'

'Oh,' said Rixon, 'right.'

'But the point is,' his mum went on, 'that I am his last remaining relative; the closest one, anyway.'

Her eyes were fixed on him now, and her hands reached forward to grab hold of his fingers. Rixon couldn't remember the last time he'd seen his mother so intense. But she didn't look scared; now she looked excited.

'So . . . ?' Rixon ventured. His mum's nails were

actually starting to pinch his skin.

'So that's why we are going to meet the lawyer tomorrow.'

From the moment she swept out of Rixon's bedroom, to the point when they boarded the train the next morning, to the very second when they stood outside the grand old brick building, there had been absolutely no mention from his mum that it was Thursday. She'd not referred once to the fact that Rixon was missing a day of school.

Rixon, of course, hadn't breathed a word about it. He didn't want to jinx it. But now he was starting to get worried. This was thrilling but it was also weird.

He looked at his mum. She was wearing a long red skirt he'd never seen before and a green jacket with a shiny gold brooch. She looked, he thought, a bit like an upside-down traffic light. But he didn't mention it. His mum was glaring at a piece of paper in her hand and comparing it to a list of names inscribed on metal plates screwed to the front door.

Rixon checked his reflection in the adjoining window. His pale brown hair was behaving better than normal; it had responded to furious combing before they left, but there was a curl at the front which always refused to stay flat. He couldn't see his freckles, but he knew they were there. According to Baz Khan at school, there were 101 on his nose alone, so he'd started calling Rixon 'Dalmatian'. Apparently, it was a Disney film about spotty dogs. Rixon thought there could be worse nicknames.

'Rixon, stop dreaming! Come on, we are going in.'

His mum grabbed the sleeve of Rixon's jumper with her left hand while simultaneously pressing a buzzer with her right. The huge wooden front door clicked open, and Rixon just had time to glance at the name alongside the button his mum had pressed before she dragged him through the entrance.

'Arnold Crump', Rixon read. He thought it was an odd name.

Rixon, in fact, only had a vague idea about what lawyers actually did. He had no concept whatsoever that Arnold Crump was about to change his life.

'Good day, good day, young Mr Webster. And may I thank you for making the journey,' the man said from his seat behind a huge wooden desk, as they entered his office.

He looked, if Rixon was trying to put it kindly, unique. His face was lined and scrunched like screwed-up newspaper, and he was completely bald except for a dozen strands of white hair which sprouted from his scalp like question marks. But even stranger, he only seemed to want to talk to Rixon. He was ignoring Rixon's mum completely.

'I hope you're not missing too much on a school day,' Mr Crump continued. 'I always enjoyed Wednesdays, as we'd be permitted to use the main playing field for athletics. I hope you're not being denied a similar activity this sunny Wednesday afternoon, Rixon?'

'It's Thursday,' Rixon replied.

'Ah! It is? Oh, of course, it is.' Mr Crump leaned back in his chair and let out a guffaw which quickly became a coughing fit.

'Ahem!' Rixon's mum cleared her throat pointedly, when the din from behind the desk had subsided. 'Could we perhaps get on with this?'

She was wearing her fierce look, Rixon saw. Mr Crump noticed it too.

'Ah, yes, indeed, Mrs Webster,' The lawyer produced a pair of wire-framed spectacles from the breast pocket of his blazer and leaned forward slowly in his chair. 'Of course, you had to come as well.'

'I am here because you wrote to me.' Rebecca Webster replied frostily, 'I am here to find out what my dear uncle left me in his will, and I would sincerely like you to hurry up.'

'Forgive me,' Mr Crump said, as his glasses fell from his nose into a half-drunk cup of tea on the desk.

At that point, for a few minutes, the entertainment ended. Rixon tried to concentrate on the conversation between his mum and the lawyer but Mr Crump droned on with lots of long sentences which began with the words 'legally speaking'.

Rixon's ears pricked up when Mr Crump explained that his great-uncle Silvester had been some sort of explorer, who 'probably made his money discovering jewels and relics . . . although nobody really knows'. Rixon also grasped that Silvester had met his death in a 'boating accident', which sounded intriguing.

But his mum wanted to know something

else, desperately. 'Can we please,' she said, just managing to control her frustration, 'get to the will?'

Arnold Crump looked at Rixon's mum and nodded slowly. He then turned his head towards Rixon, nodded solemnly again, and then finally looked down at a piece of paper on the desk in front of him. The lawyer cleared his throat.

'At the time of his death,' Mr Crump said slowly, 'Silvester Rixon was a millionaire. To be precise, he was more than that. He was—if you like—a millionaire two and half times over.'

Rixon's mum gasped so loudly Rixon reached out to grab her arm in alarm. He feared she might faint. Rixon knew that happened when people got a shock. He was feeling very light-headed himself.

'Two . . . and a half . . . MILLION?!' his mum spluttered.

'Indeed,' Mr Crump replied, 'and all of it was to go to one beneficiary when he died—his will is very clear about that . . .'

'Yes,' Rixon's mother said, already nodding her head enthusiastically.

'All the money has been left—' Mr Crump continued.

'To his closest living relative, his niece, Rebecca

Webster,' finished Rixon's mum.

Mr Crump, however, ignored her and kept on reading the sheet of paper in front of him. 'The money has been left,' he said firmly, 'to the North Niblington Society of Seagull Supporters.'

'Wh-what?!' stammered Rixon's mother.

'They have been advised,' Mr Crump went on, 'to use the funds—in part—to pay for a floating gull hospital, if this is feasible. This new facility will rescue any bird which is injured out at sea.'

Rixon's mum was staring at Mr Crump with her mouth open. Rixon could see her tongue poised midway between her lips, but she was making no sound. Her arms hung motionless in front of her, frozen like a statue trying to catch a ball.

'I take it, Mrs Webster, this was possibly not the news you were expecting?' Mr Crump suggested.

Rixon's mum had turned ghostly pale. She'd seen a small fortune placed right in front of her . . . and then watched it disappear in a puff of smoke.

'A gull hospital? A floating gull hospital? A hospital for birds? In the sea?' she whispered.

'Quite so,' said Mr Crump, who almost looked sorry for her. 'An idea that's ingenious, innovative, and, dare I suggest, almost completely pointless.'

Rixon was wondering what a seagull hospital might actually look like. Would there be gull doctors scouring the ocean nearby for stricken birds? Would they use jet skis?

His mother, however, was now turning towards the door.

'Come on, Rixon,' she said, grabbing her son's arm, 'let's go. I'm afraid this has been a complete waste of time.'

But the lawyer, in fact, was not finished. 'Mrs Webster, I urge you—in fact, I *instruct* you—to remain here until I complete the reading of the will. Or, if you insist on leaving, please allow Rixon to remain. It is vital that he hears what I have to say.'

Rixon planted his feet on the office floor and spun his head back round to the desk. 'What,' he said, 'me?'

Mr Crump nodded more solemnly than ever. Rixon removed his mum's hand from his arm.

'Rixon, do you fully understand what a will is?' Mr Crump was creaking his way to his feet as he spoke.

'Yes, of course,' Rixon answered. 'I mean, it's what people decide to do with their money when they're not here. When they're, well, dead.'

Mr Crump nodded, finally upright. Rixon was astonished to see him at his full height: the old man must have been almost seven feet tall, and the strands of hair on his head nearly brushed the ceiling.

'You're right, Rixon,' Mr Crump said, 'but you're also wrong. What we are discussing here is not money. It's something far more valuable than that.'

Rixon was vaguely aware of his mother groaning alongside him. 'Only rich people think there's something more valuable than money . . .' Rixon heard her say. But Arnold Crump was not distracted.

'A will distributes possessions, Rixon. The deceased person decides who gets what, you understand?'

Rixon nodded; of course he understood.

'So, Rixon, I am hereby informing you that officially, that is to say legally, you now own . . .'

'Yes?' Rixon encouraged him. He was thinking his great-uncle, having been an explorer, could have left him a telescope. He'd often wanted one.

Mr Crump took one final deep breath, fixed his gaze directly at Rixon, and said, '. . . an island.'

There was a second of silence before Rixon's

brain found a word in response.

'What?' he murmured in disbelief. He felt certain he must have misheard, or that Crump was joking. But the lines on the old man's face were not turning into a smile.

'What?' his mum added in a louder voice.

'An island?' Rixon repeated, still expecting the lawyer to start laughing.

But Mr Crump was utterly serious. 'Quite so, an island,' he confirmed.

The lawyer was now reaching into a drawer on his side of the desk. He pulled out a large sheet of tatty paper and slowly started to unroll it. He placed a vase of dead flowers on one end and a huge dictionary on the other, to keep the sheet flat. Then he beckoned to Rixon. 'Come round so you can see it better.'

The markings were very faint and the paper itself was yellowed and torn in several places, but Rixon knew what it was.

'A map,' Rixon said, 'it's a map. But it looks really old . . .'

'This map was drawn up in 1792,' Mr Crump confirmed. 'It is extremely rare, very valuable, and, for our purposes, essential.'

Rixon watched carefully as Mr Crump's finger

slowly moved across the map.

'Gilberton—that's where you live, isn't it, Rixon?'

He nodded. It was the only place he'd ever lived.

'Well, that's where Gilberton is, roughly,' Mr Crump said, tapping a fingernail on a blank section of the map. 'It was just fields in the eighteenth century,' he explained.

'Oh, right,' Rixon mumbled, trying to see if there was anywhere else on the map he recognized. The writing was so curled and conjoined that he couldn't really make out any of the words. The only thing that possibly made sense was a jagged outline on the far right-hand side of the map.

'Is that . . . the coast?' Rixon suggested hesitantly.

'Quite so,' Mr Crump replied, 'and that's where I need you to focus. Let's begin on the coastline and keep looking, travelling, as it were, eastwards . . . out into the sea. Now, watch closely . . .'

Mr Crump's fingernail slowly traced an imaginary diagonal path, from the thick line which marked the edge of the mainland out into the sea. And then, just before it reached the very edge of the map, the finger suddenly stopped.

'Oh, blast!' he said, 'I've lost it again.'

Crump slapped the palm of his hand on the desk in frustration, and the vibrations made something rattle on the wooden surface. Rixon reached across the width of huge desk to pick it up.

'Would this help?' he suggested, handing Mr Crump a large magnifying glass.

'Yes, perfect!' Mr Crump exclaimed. 'I must have left it there this morning, when I was trying to find the island. Now, concentrate . . .'

The lawyer bent over the map holding the magnifying glass just above it. Rixon leaned in with him. He could hear his mother sighing as she lingered by the door. But Rixon had no intention of leaving.

'Aha! Got it, got it! Now Rixon, look here!'

Mr Crump creaked to one side so that Rixon could lower his own face over the magnifying glass. Rixon studied the map with his right eye; then he closed that one and used his left instead. The result was the same. As hard as Rixon looked, all he could make out was a tiny black speck. It was shaped like a comma, all on its own, surrounded by sea. Focusing hard, Rixon could make out the faintest of lines alongside it. It was an arrow drawn in pencil running from the speck to some writing beneath.

There were two words, both still tiny even when magnified. The first one began with an 's', followed, Rixon thought, by a 'p'. The other letters were too smudged to be clear, although there seemed to be an 'r'. The second word had almost disappeared, but Rixon could make out the ending 'and'.

'S-P-R . . . AND,' he read aloud, 'and a few letters in between. It looks like it's pointing to a tiny, tiny island.'

'Yes,' said Mr Crump, 'a tiny, tiny island. So small, so insignificant, that from this date onwards it never appeared on any map ever again. But your great-uncle knew of its existence, even if no one else did, and he claimed it for his own.'

'What?' Rixon's mum said from the doorway. 'You're not serious?'

'Oh yes, quite serious,' Mr Crump replied, but he didn't turn his head towards her. He was looking straight at Rixon.

'It was his island—we have all the papers to prove it,' Mr Crump continued, 'and now . . . it's yours.'

Rixon felt his stomach suddenly lurch towards

the floor. But Mr Crump seemed perfectly calm, smiling at him, and using his most solemn lawyer's voice.

'Rixon Webster, it is my appointed duty to inform you that from this day forward, at the express wish of your great-uncle Silvester, you are the legal and rightful owner of that tiny speck of land.'

Chapter 2

For a week, his mum's answer had been simple. Every time Rixon asked the question, she'd just reply, 'No.' The thing was, Rixon could see her point, that was always his problem, he could always see other people's points. He could understand why his mum didn't want him to try to find Splinter Island. But Rixon didn't just *want* to go, he *had* to go. It was *his* place, his very own island. How could he live without at least seeing it!

The trouble was, although he'd been to the library (twice), and had searched on the Internet (every lunchtime at school), he couldn't actually find any mention of a place called 'Splinter Island'. It wasn't recorded, reported, or referenced anywhere. Mr Crump had calculated that the nearest place on the mainland to the island— or at least where the island was meant to be—

was North Niblington (the home of the seagull society, Rixon remembered with a wince). That village was actually only a couple of hours' drive from them, and his mum had a car which started perfectly (most mornings). But there was no way he could convince her to go there.

'Where's the evidence, Rixon?' she said, turning off the television. 'We've only seen one old sheet of paper from the seventeenth century . . .'

'Eighteenth century,' Rixon corrected her.

'. . . from hundreds of years ago,' she persisted, 'that *might* show vaguely where the island *might* be and then—guess what?—nothing. Nobody's seen it, visited it, heard about it, or even cared about it since.'

'Great-uncle Silvester did,' Rixon replied.

'Oh, Silvester . . .' his mum said with a sigh. 'You must understand, Rixon: Uncle Silvester was the family mystery. None of us knew where he was from one year to the next, or even from one decade to the next. He was lovely, when you saw him. But the point is, you never saw him. He was—' she made a twirling motion with her hands '—like the wind. That's it; he was like the wind. Wild and uncontrollable.'

Rixon didn't argue any more. But even when

he lay on his bed that night he could imagine that old map in front of him; he could picture its creased and stained surface. He saw that tiny island waiting for him. It had to be real.

And Rixon also had the envelope.

Mr Crump had thrust it into his hands just as Rixon had left the lawyer's office. He'd waited until his mum wasn't looking. 'Silvester's final instruction was that you were to have this,' Crump had whispered. 'I don't know what's inside,' he'd added.

Well, Rixon did know. He'd opened the envelope as soon as he'd got home. He spread it all out in front of him again now on the bed and tried to make sense of it. It was extremely confusing.

There were lots of newspaper cuttings, mainly front pages, dating from five years before. They were all about the same story. A group of scientists, described by some as 'mega boffins', had gone missing. They'd stolen secret information, vital to the country's future, and run off with it. Nobody knew where they'd gone— they just seemed to have vanished into thin air. One of the papers described it as 'The Great Science Scandal!'; another called the scientists 'traitors'. It was interesting, certainly, but Rixon had no idea what it had got to do with him or Splinter Island.

Then there was the memory stick. This had been tucked inside the envelope too, and it provided another, different mystery. Carefully, Rixon reached under his bed for his most prized possession—the laptop computer his dad had given him for his birthday. The laptop computer his mum still didn't know about. Rixon was worried that, if she saw it, she'd insist that they sell it. He knew their car needed a new exhaust and the washing machine had to be fixed.

But Rixon loved his laptop. He knew it wasn't the very latest generation, there were newer models in the shops, but to Rixon it could not have been more precious. It was dark red, smooth and sleek in his hands. The surface glimmered when it caught the light as he opened it up.

Best of all it was a Caiman. All his friends wanted a Caiman computer, or a Caiman phone, but even their older devices were seriously expensive. Not only did they have the best graphics and memory, but they just *looked* so good. Rixon turned the computer around in his hands and traced the outline of the logo on the lid with his finger—a silver caiman. It was like a small crocodile with an elongated tail which curled upwards and back towards the head, making the whole creature resemble the letter 'C'.

He clicked on the file he'd downloaded from the memory stick. Rixon frowned at the words. It was like another language—a series of mathematical equations and detailed instructions which he couldn't begin to interpret. There was a diagram at the bottom. It resembled a tiny shoebox but with ports and sockets at either end, as if it was designed for wires or cables to be attached to it.

Rixon spent twenty minutes searching online to see if he could find any images that matched it, or any clue about what the diagram could actually represent. There was nothing.

'But what has any of this got to do with Splinter Island?' Rixon muttered to himself as he began to shut down the computer. At that precise moment, he felt he had as much chance of visiting Jupiter as the island he supposedly now owned. Caught up in his own frustrations, it was only when he clicked to close down the homescreen that Rixon noticed the date.

'Oh no,' he whispered. It was coming, it was tomorrow: his parents' wedding anniversary.

One day of the year he knew his mum always remembered; one day when Rixon could never predict her mood. This year was no exception.

'I don't suppose your dad has phoned you, has he?' his mum inquired at breakfast.

Rixon shook his head. He couldn't actually recall the last conversation he'd had with his father. It might have been his birthday; his dad had been working abroad and had phoned from wherever he was to check that the laptop had been delivered.

'No, he didn't call me, either,' his mum continued, stirring the sugar in the cup of coffee she'd poured for herself twenty minutes before.

'Sorry,' Rixon said vaguely.

'Oh, goodness, Rixon, it's not your fault!' his mum declared, suddenly standing up from the kitchen chair. 'I don't know why I expect him to acknowledge our anniversary now. He hardly ever remembered it when we were married!'

She turned to the fridge, opened the door, and then immediately shut it again. 'So . . . anyway,' she said. 'It's Saturday tomorrow. What are your plans for the weekend, Rixy?'

He said nothing for a second, partly because he hated 'Rixy' even more than 'Rixon', but mainly because he didn't have any plans for the weekend at all. He knew Baz Khan and his dad were organizing a football match just out of town. But, considering his mum did one of her receptionist shifts every Saturday morning, Rixon knew he had no way of getting there. He didn't want to make his mum feel bad, so he said, 'I'll probably just do some homework...'

His mum picked up the coffee cup, held it to her mouth, and then put it down again. She glanced at Rixon and then looked as though she might cry. He hoped desperately that she wouldn't. Luckily, she started to smile instead.

'Saturdays shouldn't just be about homework,' she said. 'Is your life really that boring, Rixon?'

He didn't know how to answer that, so he just shrugged.

She nodded, took a sip from the coffee cup, and then suddenly turned to the sink and poured it away. 'Ugh ... cold coffee,' she said. She turned to look at him. 'I hate to see you sad,' she said quietly. 'So I've decided. But, just remember, it doesn't actually exist.'

'What—what do you mean?' Rixon said,

increasingly confused.

'The island, of course. Whatever-it's-called Island . . .'

'Splinter?'

'Yes, that. It doesn't exist. But there's only one way I'm ever going to convince you about that, isn't there, Rixon?'

Rixon's heart suddenly felt as though it would burst through his ribs as he sat at their kitchen table. He stopped chewing his toast, his mind racing to the only possible answer to his mum's question.

'By looking for it. . . ?' he whispered.

'Yes,' she said. 'We'll do it tomorrow. I'll swap shifts and work a Sunday instead, and get this nonsense over with . . .'

She was using a cross voice, but she was smiling too. Rixon jumped from his chair, punched the air, high-fived his mum so hard she almost fell over, and then ran all the way to school. It was two miles. Rixon could have sprinted twenty.

On Saturday morning, Rixon was so excited in the car, it was perhaps inevitable that the small coastal village would fail to meet his expectations.

'It's a bit bleak,' Rixon said, looking around as they parked up.

'If this is *North* Niblington, where's the rest of it?' his mum said.

What lay in front of them were two lines of grey; one being a beach of tiny pebbles and the other being the sea. It had been sunny in Gilberton, but it wasn't here. A dark cloud hung over the ocean and the water seethed with small white waves.

As soon as Rixon left the car, he felt the wind: it ruffled his hair and stung his cheeks. He zipped up his blue tracksuit top and stuffed his hands into his jeans pockets. Then the wind dropped and he immediately felt too hot. Rixon quickly turned back, opened the car door, and grabbed his rucksack. It contained a packed lunch, which his mum knew about, and his laptop, which his mum didn't know about. Rixon had shoved it in the bottom of the bag at the last minute.

'I'm going to look for a signpost,' he told his mum.

Rixon's mum had left the car but, having felt a gust of the coastal air, was now opening the door to get back in it.

'Tell me if you find a café,' was all she said in reply.

In truth, Rixon didn't know exactly what he was looking for, but after ten minutes of walking, he was certain he hadn't found it. There was no signpost with an arrow helpfully indicating the way to Splinter Island; there was no tourist information centre selling Splinter Island guidebooks. There was just a row of terraced houses set back from the beach, a convenience shop which was closed, and a kids' playground with the swings missing.

North Niblington seemed deserted.

So Rixon turned his attention to the ocean. He watched the waves scuttle towards shore in a repeating pattern, grey sea flecked with white. The same movement. The same process. There was nothing to disturb the monotonous rhythm, except the boat.

When Rixon caught sight of it he dashed forwards. Further down the beach, a jetty extended twenty metres into the sea. It was just a wooden walkway supported by a few barnacle-encrusted poles. Rixon trod carefully, as a few planks of wood were missing, but he could see clearly now. The boat was heading straight towards him.

'Wait there!' a booming voice commanded,

strong enough to reach Rixon's ears on the wind.

The boat bounced on the waves, skimming the surface of the sea. It was pale blue in colour and reminded Rixon of the rowing boats on the lake in Gilberton Park. The craft now approaching him looked as though it had space for half a dozen people. But currently it was occupied by a solitary man with a ginger-coloured beard. He was using his left hand to operate the outboard motor and the right one to wave at Rixon.

'Almost with you!' he shouted.

The booming voice seemed to have a friendly tone to it but Rixon was still confused.

He raised his own hand in a half-hearted wave back. Then, as the boat slowed and turned alongside the jetty, Rixon saw the words painted in bright red capital letters on the side: 'North Niblington Ferry'.

Now Rixon was starting to understand. This man thought Rixon was a customer.

But before Rixon could utter a word, the ginger-bearded ferryman was right in front of him. He'd secured the boat with a loose knot of rope and hauled himself onto the jetty in one fluid, rapid movement.

Now he stuck out a right hand which was the

size of a spade and as hairy as a horse's mane.

'Asa Hartley, at your service, young sir,' he said, crushing Rixon's fingers in his grip.

'Oh, hi, I am Rixon . . . Rixon Webster,' he managed to reply.

'I have previously met a few Websters, but never a Rixon,' Asa Hartley declared, releasing the handshake to Rixon's relief. 'So where can I take you?'

'Take me? On the boat you mean?'

Asa Hartley frowned at him.

'Well, I haven't got an aeroplane, as you can probably tell. And you are standing in the precise spot where customers wait for my ferry service.'

'Yes, of course, sorry,' Rixon replied, an idea suddenly sprouting and blooming in his mind, 'so, where do you actually . . . go?'

'Day trips and sightseeing a speciality,' Asa Hartley began brightly. 'Although, in truth, we don't get many holidaymakers until August. And actually, we don't get many then,' he conceded.

'Oh,' Rixon said, 'well, I'm not on holiday. I'm just here for the day, with my mum.'

'Ah, the lady walking across from the car park? Yes, I see her. Well then, I expect you'll want a quick trip across to West Warbleton? We can be across the bay in twenty minutes—'

'No, actually, I don't want to go there,' Rixon interrupted. It was obvious, the more he thought about it. The answer to all his problems was right there, literally standing in front of him!

'I want to go,' Rixon said, almost stumbling over the words in his excitement, 'I mean, I would like you to take me . . . to Splinter Island!'

Asa Hartley's eyes were denim blue and they focused on Rixon now with such an intense gaze that Rixon almost cowered. Asa Hartley stared, stunned—and for a full five seconds did not utter a sound. Then he slowly opened his mouth, tipped back his head, and released the most boisterous roar of laughter Rixon had ever heard.

'Splinter Island!' Asa Hartley bellowed. 'Splinter Island? Oh, my goodness, I'm sure I haven't heard those two words for forty years.'

He seemed almost hysterical. Rixon waited for the laughter to subside before nervously asking his next question.

'But, do you know where Splinter Island is?'

That just started him off again. Asa Hartley rocked back on his heels in a fresh fit of amusement.

'Oh my, oh my, yes, I do know where Splinter Island is, young Webster . . .'

'Yes? Yes?'

'It's in the imagination of whatever trickster made up the story in the first place. I heard it from my grandfather, but I'm certain he got it from someone else—*his* grandad, probably.'

'What do you mean, "story"?'

Asa Hartley fixed him with another denim-eyed stare. 'Well, if I remember rightly, it goes like this. It so happens, they say, that the Devil himself was set upon grabbing a whole section of this land.'

Rixon, having no idea how to respond, just nodded.

'So he made himself a chisel, fashioned from the flames of the underworld. It was a thousand feet tall and as sharp as a tiger's claw. This the Devil held in his left hand, while in his right he carried a stone the size of a cathedral, with which to bash the chisel, you see, Rixon, the Devil being a fairly large chap. With me?'

'Erm, with you,' Rixon mumbled.

'Well, the wind blew,' Asa Hartley continued, 'and not just any normal wind. It was the biggest, fullest, strongest gust of wind ever felt by man or beast since the dawning of time. And it knocked that Devil clean over, at the precise moment when he was raising that rock above the chisel to strike!'

'So his plan failed?'

'Indeed, his plan failed, Rixon, except for one little thing. One little piece. As he was falling backwards, his diabolical chisel struck the very edge of the coast. A tiny piece of rock from the cliff face was hurled out into the ocean: a splinter, you see, Rixon, a splinter.'

'And that's how the island got its name! Splinter Island!' Rixon exclaimed.

'Exactly,' said Asa Hartley with a grin. 'It's a wonderful story and also the biggest load of turnip juice. What amazes me is how you got to know about a made-up place?'

'Made-up?' Rixon answered. 'You mean Splinter Island doesn't exist? It isn't real?'

Asa Hartley gently shook his head. 'I don't exactly know what lies in your imagination, young Webster. But I need passengers requiring transportation to places that actually exist.'

With that, he turned and strode back to his boat, lowering himself onto it from the jetty. Rixon watched him pull the cord to start the outboard motor, and take hold of the tiller stick which stuck out into the boat itself. Rixon even noticed how Asa Hartley gently turned the handle of the tiller like a throttle to make the boat move.

And that should have been that. Asa Hartley and his boat should have been gone, out of sight. But something, someone, intervened in a moment which changed everything . . . although Rebecca Webster didn't realize that. All she wanted was a simple cup of coffee.

'Excuse me, excuse me!' she shouted, waving both arms above her head and making her way as fast as she could down the jetty towards Asa Hartley.

Somewhere in the corner of his eye he saw her; something in his mind made him cut the engine and turn to smile at Rixon's mum.

'Oh, thank you,' she said. 'It's just that we've had a long drive and, well, I was going to bring a flask but then I forgot . . . Is there a café anywhere around here? Of course, I'd be delighted to buy you a drink if you could show us the way,' she added. 'Coffee, or whatever . . .'

That seemed to sway it.

'Well, it's the best offer I've had today,' Asa Hartley said, already clambering back onto the jetty. 'There's a place the other side of the kiddies' playground. It's a bit early but they'll open up if I knock loud enough.'

'Great,' Rixon's mum replied. 'Come on, Rixon, I'll buy you a lemonade. At least it will be something before we go home.'

Rixon heard her but he didn't move. 'Does that mean we're giving up?' he said.

Rixon's mum sighed and placed a hand on his shoulder. 'Look, Rixy.' He flinched as he heard that horrible abbreviation. 'Rixon, darling,' his mum continued, 'I know how disappointed you must be. I am too, honestly. It would be lovely to think that there were secret islands just waiting to be discovered. I'm afraid life's not like that . . .'

'But the will . . . great-uncle Silvester,' Rixon protested.

'I think he must have lost his mind; that's the only explanation,' his mum said. 'I mean, why else would he leave his money to a seagull hospital?'

Asa Hartley was close enough to overhear. 'A seagull hospital?' he cried. 'Who would want to save seagulls? There's about a million too many of them as it is!' He gave one bemused chuckle and exchanged a smile with Rixon's mum.

So Great-uncle Silvester was mad, and the whole thing had been a crazy joke? Rixon couldn't accept it. He didn't want to accept it.

'Maybe we're just on the wrong bit of the coast,' he said, 'and we could come again next weekend?'

'Next weekend, I'll be working,' Rixon's mum replied sadly. She smoothed down the tufts of Rixon's hair. They were immediately made vertical again by the wind.

'Look, come and have a lemonade. We can even look for an ice cream,' his mum said.

Lemonade and ice cream? He wasn't six years old. Rixon felt a fury rising inside him.

'No, thanks,' he replied, 'you go. I'll just have one last look at the sea. I don't suppose we'll ever be here again.'

He stuffed his hands into his jeans pockets.

'Rixon, come on,' his mum tried.

Rixon didn't move.

'He can watch the boat for me,' Asa Hartley suggested, gesturing to the rope which hung loosely on the jetty. 'Any sign of the wind getting up and I'll need you to tighten that knot, that OK?'

The idea of a free drink had clearly taken a firm hold in Asa Hartley's mind. But a very different idea was just starting to take shape in Rixon's.

'Yes, I can do that,' Rixon replied, not knowing the first thing about knots. 'I'll stay here and get some fresh air. I've got my phone.'

'Well,' his mum hesitated. 'I do really need a coffee before I do that drive back. And, to be honest, I could use the loo as well. Look, I'll grab a takeaway. We'll only be ten minutes. Just call me if you need anything, OK?'

'I'm fine, just go!' Rixon insisted, turning his back to them.

He heard their footsteps on the pebbles, he heard their chatter fade into the distance, but Rixon's mind was in a state of revolution. The idea was so daring, so radical, it truly scared him. But now that it was lodged in his brain, Rixon could just not shake it off.

He knew he had one chance. People kept telling him his island didn't exist, but it was *his* island, a lawyer had told him that, and lawyers, he'd decided, don't joke. Plus there was the map. It might have been old, but it was real, and it showed that Splinter Island was only a few miles from where he was standing! If he didn't try to find it now then Rixon knew the opportunity would never come again.

He was alone, on a beach with a boat. And he

had seen how that boat worked.

Rixon had built his life on caution. He was a good boy, careful and responsible. That approach, he decided, had got him nowhere. It was time for a change; it was time for action.

Before he could stop himself, Rixon was inside that boat. The rope was looped around the rail of the jetty, and he untied it easily, dropping it down by his feet.

Now Rixon was desperately trying to remember the right order of things. The first job was to start the engine. The motor was like a large black box at the stern of the boat; near the top was a handle attached to a strong thread. Rixon pulled it so hard it felt like his own muscles would snap. No response. He tried even harder, then harder still. The effort was so great, Rixon almost fell backwards as his right arm recoiled, but he heard the engine coughing into life.

Now he could see a small lever on the side of the motor, he'd watched Asa Hartley adjust it. It could be pushed forwards or pulled backwards. Logic told Rixon he needed to go forwards, so that's what Rixon did, he nudged the lever away from him and he was in gear.

Then take hold of the tiller . . . left hand . . . stay

strong. Rixon squeezed gently and turned the top of the stick towards him. This was the throttle which would set the boat on its way, and it worked, it actually worked—he was moving!

Rixon could feel the motion of the boat beneath him as he sat on the bench nearest to the motor, but he had to steer. The boat had to go towards Rixon's right, out into the open sea. So he moved the tiller that way.

'No!' Rixon yelled as the bow of the craft rotated instead back towards the jetty! Frantically he pulled the tiller back the other way.

'Come on!' Rixon cried. Now the boat was turning, but this time in the right direction.

'It goes in opposites,' Rixon told himself. The tiller controlled the boat, but pulling it left meant going right, and right meant left. Right now, he just had to keep it straight. He pulled the throttle, twisting the top of the tiller; the engine responded and the boat almost leapt forwards.

Rixon felt the first fountain of water on his face as the pointed bow of the little blue boat cut into the sea. He felt a wave of pure exhilaration as the wind bruised his cheeks and stung his eyes. He felt the muscles of his legs tense and his toes curl inside his soggy trainers as he tried to ride the bounce and descent of the boat's movement.

Rixon also thought he might have heard shouts and screams from the shore behind him. But he couldn't look back. Rixon Webster was certain of one thing: he'd taken the most monumental decision of his life and he couldn't look back.

Chapter 3

For the first fifteen minutes, Rixon was captivated by his new role as ship's captain. He'd found a bright orange life jacket stuffed beneath the bench where he sat and the feel of that around his chest made him even more confident. His vessel was like a puppet, responding to his every touch. He was quickly learning to predict the motion of the boat over the waves, feeling it with his legs rather than fighting it. He was riding the surf. His touch on the tiller was light but sure; if he wanted the boat to go left, it did, and likewise with right.

But then Rixon began to feel sick. He tried to blame it on the sea. In truth, he knew it was something else. Guilt was beginning to overwhelm him. He had never stolen anything before. Now he had taken a boat, an actual boat, and he no idea where he was even taking it. He was in the middle of the sea, the huge, monstrous, actual, grey sea!

'It's not my fault!' Rixon yelled above the chug of the motor and the churn of the waves to no one in particular. He hadn't asked to see that old lawyer; he hadn't asked to be given an island!

But that was the reality; those things had happened. And now he, Rixon Webster, was trying to honour the dying wish of his great-uncle. Nobody else was going to help, that much was clear. He had to do it alone. And besides, he assured himself, he would return the boat very soon. As long as he didn't run out of fuel.

The arguments raged inside Rixon's head as the boat ploughed forwards. But eventually Rixon came to a decision. It was the obvious one, the only one. He was turning back.

He would have to accept the fury of his mother, never mind the anger of Asa Hartley. Just thinking about this made him feel so weak that his head fell down towards his chest.

But when Rixon looked up again, he saw it.

It was just an outline really, a thin dark line. At first, Rixon thought it could have been the horizon; then he thought it could be a big ship in the distance; but he soon decided it was neither. Rixon was intrigued, his imagination was sparked again. His life, he reasoned, would barely be worth living when he got back to the shore, so he might as well use another few minutes of it on the boat.

With as much bravery as he could summon, Rixon twisted the throttle, wiped a strand of wet hair from his eye, and tried to focus on what lay ahead.

He was approaching a wall of rock. It stuck out of the sea like a miniature mountain, dull grey in colour, stretching upwards roughly to the height of a house. Rixon didn't know why it was there, but then, why were rocks anywhere? The waves reared and crashed onto it, while Rixon stared at it, his mind spinning.

'Is that it?' he asked aloud. 'Is that all?'

Was this his island? The prized possession he'd risked so much to reach? Rixon felt a pang of excitement followed by disappointment. If that was all Splinter Island amounted to, then no wonder people had forgotten about it. It looked dangerous to go much closer and there was not really any point. There was nothing more to see.

Until Rixon spotted the gulls.

He'd been accompanied by a couple of birds throughout the journey, but they hadn't bothered him, and he hadn't really paid them much attention. Even though Rixon lived a decent distance from the coast, he was well used to seagulls—they were always in the playground, chasing apple cores or sandwich crusts.

But suddenly there were seagulls everywhere— twenty now, no, fifty. More were arriving all the time. It became impossible to count them all.

They swooped from the sky in groups, wings outstretched, gliding on the currents of wind until they became a cloud of feathers, circling and hovering.

There was something else too, something which felt wrong. Rixon realized that all these birds, hundreds and hundreds of them gathered together, were all silent. It was so quiet the whistle sounded like an explosion.

It was the noise a referee would use to start a match or a teacher to break up a schoolyard fight. But now, in the middle of the ocean, it was the sound which summoned the seagulls. They responded with a noise beyond Rixon's imagination.

The cry from a thousand seagulls sounded

like the screech of a thousand trains braking suddenly on their tracks, a piercing, ripping, scream. It was as if a street of smoke alarms had suddenly been activated. Rixon covered his ears with his hands, but his eyes were wide open. The gulls were starting to do something utterly astonishing.

In unison, they turned in flight so the tips of their bills were facing the very top of the wall of rock. And then they bit it. They truly bit the rock.

At first, Rixon thought there must be some kind of food sprinkled on top, and that maybe this was a bizarre feeding ritual. But if there was food there, it was taking them an awfully long time to eat it. And all the gulls were still in the same position. Their wings were flapping but their bills seemed to be stuck, clasped on the very surface of the rock, right at its summit, some thirty metres above Rixon's head. The birds were not moving.

But the rock was.

Rixon released the tiller and grabbed the edge of his seat, as if he needed to touch something solid, to believe he wasn't dreaming. His brain could not accept what his eyes were telling him: the wall of rock was now moving.

Slowly, right in front of him, a small gap emerged. The one wall of rock was actually becoming two. Half of the rock face was inching its way towards the left, the other half slowly moving to the right, leaving a space in the middle.

Still the gulls remained in their perfect line, stretched out across the summit. But Rixon wasn't concentrating on them any more; something else had suddenly grabbed all his attention.

There was something behind the wall. Something which was slowly being revealed.

The boat crept forwards at Rixon's touch. The waves chopped and chased around it, but Rixon was oblivious to everything except what he saw in front of him.

Behind the wall of rock there was land and the sight of it made Rixon gasp more deeply than ever. He could now see, unmistakeably, an island—a proper island.

Immediately in front of him there was a beach of sand and stones; behind that was a copse of tall trees. The whole thing was only a little larger than a football pitch, but it was there!

A *splinter* of land, hidden from the rest of the world. It seemed impossible. And yet he was looking at it, it was right in front of him!

As the boat passed through the gap in the wall of rock, Rixon noticed that the sea calmed, as though the island was encircled by its own lagoon. But there was something else which made Rixon's mind wobble and his heart leap all over again.

There were huge metal poles rising from the surface of the water. They were like pieces of rusting scaffolding which, in turn, supported a thinner rail above them. This curved section of metal appeared to run all the way around the top of the wall. Except that Rixon was now starting to think it wasn't a wall at all. From this position, on the other side of it, he could see it had no thickness. What's more, it didn't even look like rock. What it looked like, Rixon suddenly realized, was an enormous, filthy, grey set of curtains.

He was close enough to reach out as he passed, and what he touched confirmed his suspicions. His fingers did not feel the cold, solid surface of a rock face. What he touched was canvas. The whole thing was a massive expanse of material, painted to look like a wall of rock if anyone happened to approach it from the open sea but revealed now to be nothing more than a façade.

It was, indeed, the most stupendous set

of curtains. The seagulls, in their multitudes, with their combined strength and relentless organization, had opened them for him.

All the different emotions which had swirled inside Rixon over the past hour were now replaced by simple, soaring, excitement.

Within a minute, he'd reached the shore of the island. Gingerly, Rixon clambered out of the boat, shuffling to the side, and then lowering himself into the shallow water. It felt as though he was going to fall; his whole body seemed to be lurching from one side to another, like he'd just come off a rollercoaster.

He steadied himself and looked around. The beach was a mixture of pale brown sand and grey stones, but the interior of the island seemed completely wild and overgrown. The skyline was dominated by what looked like a dozen huge Christmas trees. But to get to them, Rixon would have to fight through a barrier of thick bushes two metres high. It was almost like another wall, this time of thick vegetation.

This wasn't, Rixon admitted to himself, the kind of paradise island he'd secretly been imagining ever since that meeting in the lawyer's office. There wasn't a palm tree in sight. But, he told himself, that didn't matter. The point was, he was now walking with his own footsteps on his very own island. What would his mum say about that when she told him?

'So why don't I tell her, right now!' Rixon said excitedly.

He dropped the rucksack he'd carried from the boat and reached into the side pocket. The phone was there, and it was dry. That was good. But when Rixon looked at the screen, he saw there was barely a bar of network coverage and, worse still, his battery was down to 3 per cent. Silently cursing himself for watching videos on the car journey from Gilberton, Rixon selected his mum's number. He held the phone to his ear; nothing.

'Please, come on,' Rixon urged the phone, willing it to work. The fourth time he tried the number, he heard it ring, just once. His mother answered immediately.

'Rixon! For mercy's sake, where—'

'Mum? Mum? Hello?'

'. . . the boat, and then we . . . Hello? Rixon, where—?'

'Mum, I can't hear you. It keeps breaking up, but—'

'Can you speak louder? The line, Rixon . . . it's bad . . . I need to know—'

'Mum? Mum? Are you there? Mum, I've got to tell you—'

'. . . completely worried sick . . .'

'It's OK! Mum, listen, I am completely OK! And I've found it, I've actually found it!'

'What, Rixon? What are you talking about?'

'Splinter Island, I've found Splinter Island! I'm on it, right now!'

The phone whined and crackled in Rixon's ear and then fell silent.

'Mum! Mum! Did you hear me?'

When Rixon looked at the screen, he only saw his reflection. The battery was gone and with it, Rixon realized, his contact with the outside world. In his life Rixon had often felt lonely but now—for the first time—he was completely on his own.

As he pressed the power button on his phone with no effect, Rixon was vaguely aware of a huge white cloud forming and then dispersing above him. When he looked out to sea, the ocean had disappeared. Silently and efficiently, while Rixon had been trying to speak to his mum, the seagulls had closed the wall again.

Rixon had discovered Splinter Island and almost instantly had become trapped on it. His skin was prickling and his heart racing, but not with excitement. Now Rixon was starting to panic.

'Think!' he shouted in frustration.

Rixon's biggest asset, he reasoned, was the boat. It would take him back to the mainland. The problem was the wall—it was the barrier between him and the open sea. Rixon had no idea why the gulls had opened it and no way of knowing if or when they'd do it again.

But if it was only made of canvas, then perhaps he could cut a hole in it, big enough for the boat? It seemed possible. He didn't have a knife so what he needed was a stick, the biggest, sharpest stick he could find.

'Right,' Rixon said sternly to himself, 'stay calm, stay strong, and head for the trees.'

With a new sense of purpose, Rixon set off towards the middle of the island, but after twenty paces, he was face to face with a thick, tangled mass of green tendrils and brambles that seemed to grow in every direction.

Rixon took a step forward and felt a sharp prick to his leg as the thorns pierced his trousers.

He reached with his left hand to grab a branch and pull himself clear, but the next step was just as bad. With his legs stuck in the brambles, Rixon lunged forward to pull away a screen of leaves and twigs in front of him. It took all his strength, and the branches cut into his hands as Rixon tore at them in a desperate attempt to move forwards.

He gripped hard, pulled, and then suddenly, to his amazement, it gave way! A shower of leaves, sticks, and bracken fell around Rixon, and in front of him, there was empty space. It was a clearing, a bare patch of earth which had been protected by the wall of vegetation Rixon had broken through.

But Rixon didn't care much about the bare earth, and had little time to ponder the nature and the purpose of the vegetation. He was occupied with something far more urgent.

Something, or someone, was trying to kill him.

Chapter 4

A spear landed just a metre from Rixon's feet. A second came down with a thud, further to the right. The third arrived with a whistling scream and embedded itself in the ground inches from where he stood. And the fourth was the closest, landing just millimetres from Rixon's left foot.

'You missed!' yelled a boy's voice.

'Of course I missed,' answered a girl.

'We were supposed to miss, remember?' another girl said. 'That was the whole idea!'

'Hmm, well, it was still a rubbish throw by Rose. I mean, I got loads nearer.'

Frozen to the spot, Rixon looked up. He tilted his neck and turned his eyes from the spears stuck in the earth in front of him, still quivering with the vibrations of their impact, to see the four people who'd thrown them.

'Stay there!' shouted a boy.

Rixon nodded. He wondered briefly where he could possibly go, anyway.

The four children stood on a wooden platform halfway up a tree, directly in front of Rixon but on the other side of the clearing. The boy who had ordered Rixon not to move had long, fair hair which hung down to his shoulders. He was wearing a red T-shirt and was staring fiercely.

To his left was a girl of similar height, who also had long hair but copper-coloured. Her T-shirt was black, and her expression was inquisitive.

To the boy's right was another girl, the tallest of the group. Her skin was darker and her hair was a high Afro. She wore what looked like a man's striped shirt with the sleeves rolled up. She was smiling.

The final member of the group stood a little way back and he was shorter than all the others. He wore a navy blue baseball cap and oval-framed sunglasses. As a result, Rixon had no idea what the boy was thinking. But he was in no doubt about what he'd discovered.

This island, his island, was already occupied. Not only that, but everyone living here seemed perfectly capable of harming him. It was already overwhelming. And now the inhabitants were coming to confront him.

The four children descended rapidly. Rixon didn't see how they made their way down from the tree but they did it in seconds. Now they were collecting their spears right in front of him. The copper-haired girl marched across to the weapon which had landed furthest away from Rixon and threw him the quickest of glances as she bent to pick it up.

The others collected their spears and then stood motionless, uncertain what to do or say next. They were staring at Rixon with a mixture of amazement and fury. The blond-haired boy, in particular, looked as if he was ready to attack at any moment. He leaned forwards like a runner awaiting the starting gun, his face locked in a scowl.

Rixon was outnumbered and overpowered. He watched, helpless, as the tall girl took a purposeful stride towards him. It was only when they were almost nose to nose that she stopped, shifted the spear into her left hand, and held out her right.

Tentatively Rixon responded. The girl, relieved that Rixon actually knew how to shake hands,

grabbed his right with hers. Her grip rivalled Asa
Hartley's. She nodded, smiled, and said, 'Hello,
welcome to Splinter Island. Who are you and
why are you here?'

Rixon opened his mouth to answer. But
another voice spoke first.

'Whoever you are, go away.'

'Oh, shut up, Thorn, give him a chance.'

'A chance to do what? To cut us into a million
pieces?'

'Don't be so stupid—cut us? With what? He
hasn't even got a spear.'

The fair-haired boy and the copper-haired
girl were shouting at each other, while the tall
girl rolled her eyes at Rixon. 'Sorry about them,'
she said. 'I don't think you will cut us up into a
million pieces. But also I don't think you should
be here. I'd be quite happy to throw you back in
the sea. So you'd better start talking.' The girl
smiled again, raising the spear in her left hand
just high enough for Rixon to see that it was
pointing at his throat.

Rixon felt sick. But he had to speak, and he
had to say something that *meant* something.
Who they were, why they were here, Rixon had
no idea. But he knew he had to impress this

audience immediately.

'OK, hi. Hi, everyone. No, I'm not going to cut anything . . . unless you've got a cake! Ha ha!' Rixon giggled hysterically. Nobody joined in. 'Ah, OK, sorry. Well,' he began again, 'my name is Rixon Webster. I live in Gilberton. I am the great-nephew of Silvester Rixon and—' Rixon gulped for air before he finished his sentence with the words he knew to be true '—I own this island.'

The atmosphere was suddenly like a tennis match when the champion hits a smash straight into the net; there was a stunned silence. The boy with the long blond hair was the first to speak. 'Ha! Told you. He's dangerous. He's here to get us, to trick us, to riddle us. Throw him in the sea!'

'No, Thorn, didn't you hear him? He knows Silvester. He's part of his family,' Copper-hair Girl responded.

The boy was having none of it. 'Yes, I heard him. I heard him say he owns us. He wants to get us. He wants to riddle us.'

'Shush, Thorn, shut up, please.' The tall girl was now pointing her spear towards the blond-haired boy, Rixon was relieved to see. 'He didn't say he owns us. He says he owns the island. Which is different. But is still bad.' She turned back towards Rixon. 'We don't need these. Well, not for now.'

She held her spear out in front of her so that the tip pointed up towards the sky. Copper Hair and Long Blond Hair did the same. The fourth member of the group, who had said nothing at all so far, strode quickly between them, taking the weapons and putting them in a pile with his own.

'We will leave those here and go to the beach, to talk,' the tall girl pronounced decisively.

They followed her. They sat alongside her on the ground, forming a line of four in front of Rixon, who sank down before them. He was at their mercy. And the tall girl with the Afro was clearly in charge.

'My name's Faith,' she said, 'Silvester named me that because he said my smile gave him faith in himself and faith in the future.' She smiled. Rixon nervously forced a smile in return.

Next to speak was Copper Hair, who'd thrown her spear the furthest from Rixon. 'My name's Rose,' she said, 'because of my hair. It's really copper, not red, but "Copper" isn't a good name, and roses are red, so Silvester called me "Rose". I've never seen a rose. Well, not that I can remember. But I suppose he is right.'

Rixon struggled to follow the logic of this explanation but he smiled enthusiastically. This girl had seemed the least inclined to actually kill him with a spear, so he was keen to be friendly towards her.

'And my name is Thorn,' the blond boy barked out like a challenge, 'because every rose needs to be protected. That's what Silvester said. Thorns are sharp. Thorns can cut you . . .'

Rixon nodded. He knew what thorns were and he already had a very clear idea what this boy was.

'Those two are twins,' Faith now said, to Rixon's amazement.

'Oh?' he said.

'The least identical twins in history,' Faith added. 'That's what Silvester says. And that just leaves Russell.' Faith motioned her hand to her right. The boy in the navy blue baseball cap pushed back his sunglasses so they sat right on the bridge of his nose. 'Silvester says he is our museum, our keeper of records and stories,' Faith explained. 'He is called Russell because Silvester once went to a museum in London on Russell Street.'

'*Great* Russell Street,' Russell corrected her in a voice which was, to Rixon's surprise, deep and resonant. But it was soon clear Russell wasn't going to say anything else; in fact, none of the island's inhabitants were going to say a word more. They just fixed their eyes on Rixon. It was his turn.

'Look,' he began, 'I am not here to cause trouble. I only came here, to Splinter Island, for a look round really. Nobody told me there was anyone living here. I mean, I didn't want to disturb you.'

'Huh!' Thorn grunted. 'Well, it's a bit late to be saying that now, isn't it?'

'Yes, it is,' Faith agreed, 'the first golden rule— it's been broken.'

'But it's not Rixon's fault—you can't actually blame him,' Rose said. 'I mean, you let him in, Faith. You blew the whistle.'

'Yes, but golden rules are still golden rules,' Faith declared. 'We all know that.'

'Well, I don't . . .' Rixon protested.

'That's true,' Rose nodded. 'You can't break the golden rules if you don't know them.'

'Riddles,' Thorn moaned.

But Faith motioned her hand towards Russell. He pushed his sunglasses into position and slowly raised his right index finger. 'Golden rule number one, as decreed by Silvester: the children of Splinter Island must never be seen.'

'Well, yes, all right. I know that,' said Rose, 'but the point is, he has seen us, hasn't he? I mean—look—he's right there in front of us. Because you blew the whistle for the seagulls!'

Faith conceded that point with an inclination of her head. Then she turned back to Rixon. 'Who told you about Splinter Island? Nobody, absolutely nobody, is supposed to know we are here.'

'Look, it wasn't my idea,' Rixon began desperately, 'it was the lawyer's. He was the one—he told me Great-uncle Silvester had left all his cash to some crazy seagull people in his will and left the island to me; so, I mean, what could I do about it? How was I supposed to know what was going to happen after he was dead?'

Rixon looked frantically between them. But the inhabitants of Splinter Island were suddenly as silent as the stones on the beach. The waves lapped onto the shore, the wind teased the tops of the fir trees, and finally it was Rose who spoke in a faltering voice. 'Dead?' she said. 'Did you say Silvester is dead? Are you sure?'

Rixon had learned very little from his time on Splinter Island so far, very little apart from fear and bewilderment. But he had gathered that Silvester meant something to these people—something powerful.

Rixon cleared his throat and tried to speak gently. 'I am afraid, what I was told, I mean . . . what they said to me . . . yes. Yes, Rose, Silvester is dead.'

'Rubbish! Riddles! Nonsense!' Thorn threw himself up onto his feet. For a second, Rixon thought he was going to charge straight at him. But Thorn kicked the sand with one bare foot and furiously flailed his arms towards the sun. He opened his mouth to shout again—Rixon flinched in anticipation—but no words came. Then Thorn just turned and ran.

The attack, in fact, came from the sky.

The bird which swooped down towards Rixon was bigger than any he'd set eyes on before. He only glimpsed it before he frantically covered his face with his arms to try to protect himself. But Rixon could see it was shaped like an enormous gull, only it was dark, almost black. This bird was like a huge raven, sweeping, soaring and, most astonishing of all—Rixon now realized—

communicating.

The bird had quickly turned away from Rixon and was circling above Rose. It emitted a full scale of sounds; low and grumbling to begin with, building to a high-pitched squeal like a dog yelping in distress. Rose was listening intently to every note and tone. She was listening as if she understood.

'Thanks, Danny!' Rose shouted up into the sky. Then she raised her right arm above her head and, to Rixon's amazement, began to make her own series of growls and screeches which mimicked the seagull's cry. *Caa-wooor-yerp!* Rose finished in a flourish.

Danny seemed to comprehend, or at least he took that as a cue to stretch his enormous wings and head off.

'Rose, did you just talk to that bird, I mean, actually talk to it?' Rixon asked, barely believing what he'd just witnessed. But Rose ignored him. Her face was fixed in concentration. She marched towards Faith and nodded.

Faith responded immediately. 'Quick, to your positions!' she shouted. 'Thorn, grab spears and then . . .'

'Guard the beach, I know,' Thorn replied,

sprinting back towards the interior. He quickly re-emerged, holding two spears in each hand and grinning broadly.

Rose, meanwhile, had disappeared. Rixon spun around, trying to spot her, and found she was already halfway up a tree trunk. The birch tree stood at the top of the beach and Rose was climbing it like a squirrel, her hands and feet working in a perfect sequence, like she was crawling vertically. Rose stopped briefly, grabbed something that was hidden by a branch, and then continued upwards at the same speed.

'She's carrying a telescope,' Rixon whispered, as Rose disappeared among the foliage at the top of the tree.

'Of course,' Russell answered and then turned and marched towards the centre of the island, the back of his blue cap was the last thing Rixon saw amongst the green of the dense vegetation.

Faith, for her part, seemed to have vanished too. Until Rixon heard a bush talking to him, in Faith's voice.

'Danny has raised the alarm,' it said.

'What?' Rixon managed to reply.

'Danny, the leader of the seagulls, Silvester's absolute favourite. He is our lookout, Rixon,' the voice went on. 'He warns us when something strange comes near. He can see for miles, much further than we can. And he tells us, or he tells Rose. She has the gift of seagull-speaking,' the voice explained.

'Oh,' was all Rixon managed to say in response. He was immediately interrupted by a shout from the sky.

'It's him again! It's Angry Potato Man! He's back, in his massive yacht,' Rose yelled.

Rixon's two feet may been planted firmly on the beach but he felt dizzy when he saw her. Rose had extended a ladder which must have been hidden in the uppermost branches and attached to the tree trunk. Now she stood on the top rung, her left hand reaching downwards to hold herself steady but her right hand holding the telescope to her eye. She swayed like a flag at the top of a pole. Crucially, Rixon realized, the precarious position would allow Rose to just see over the top of the wall which encircled the island to the sea beyond it.

'I recognize it, it's definitely the same one,' Rose called down.

'Are you sure?' the bush shouted back.

'Yes!'

'Well, stay as low as you can, or else they'll see you!'

Rixon heard the bush sigh deeply. 'What exactly is going on?' he asked.

'Rixon, get down here!' the bush hissed back at him, 'You must make yourself invisible!'

So Rixon found himself lying face down on the ground next to a talking bush. It was completely ridiculous. But then again, in the past hour of his life, he'd not witnessed a single thing that was remotely normal.

The bush, meanwhile, was explaining. 'Rose has spotted the danger. Thorn is preparing to fight the danger. Russell has hidden from the danger.'

Slowly Faith rose to her feet. She had covered herself in an old blanket which was decorated with hundreds of leaves. Crouching down, she resembled a bush. Now, in her upright position, she looked very much like a girl wearing a leafy cloak.

'My job is to remain camouflaged so that I can negotiate with the intruders if fighting them fails,' Faith explained. 'That means talking to them, Rixon. That's what leaders do. They negotiate.'

'Faith, I thought he'd gone past,' Rose shouted down from the treetop, 'but now the yacht is turning . . . hang on, it's going in a circle. I think he's turning back. He's looking for something. Angry Potato Man is actually on the deck. I can see him!'

'Rose, be careful!'

As ridiculous as Faith looked, as crazy as the whole thing seemed, Rixon knew it wasn't a game. Splinter Island's residents were guarding themselves from something they truly feared.

'Who is Angry Potato Man?' Rixon said. He found he was whispering.

Faith looked as though she didn't want to answer. Eventually she sighed and replied, 'We call him that because he doesn't have any hair on his head and because he always looks angry. He used to come past in his big boat all the time. But we've not seen him for ages.'

'Faith, I think it's OK . . .' Rose called down. 'He's turned back towards the mainland.'

Faith blew out her cheeks in relief and began to remove her camouflage cloak. The certainty returned to her voice. 'Well, whatever he's looking for, he won't find us,' she said, smiling. 'The island is protected and hidden. That's how

Silvester made it.'

'Silvester made it?' Rixon replied, astonished by this revelation, and then amazed to find Rose by his side too, brushing a few stray leaves from her copper-coloured hair. She must have climbed down the tree in five seconds flat.

'The curtains,' Rose said. 'Silvester, and his friends, of course—they built them to keep the island hidden; to keep us hidden.'

Faith's attitude had changed again. Now that one threat had passed, she was concentrating on the next, namely, Rixon. She towered over him with her long arms folded.

'Yes, hidden,' she reflected, 'to protect us, from everyone. Which brings me back to the question of you, Rixon. Silvester has gone but you are here.'

The tone in her voice alarmed Rixon, she sounded menacing.

'But hang on, Faith,' Rixon replied, remembering something Rose had said earlier, 'you blew the whistle, didn't you?'

It was Rose who offered an explanation. 'When Silvester trained the gulls, he used a special whistle to control them,' Rose began. 'He told me he used to put food on the top of the curtains at first, you know, to attract them. Then they'd just hear the whistle and come anyway. Gulls are the cleverest of all creatures, Rixon. Silvester used to tell me they were the "sheepdogs of the sky". What's a sheepdog, Rixon?'

'Well, I—'

'That doesn't matter,' Faith said sharply. 'The point is, when Silvester went away on his trip, he entrusted me with the whistle. When Rose saw Rixon's little boat from the lookout position, I judged it to be harmless, and I reckoned a small boy couldn't hurt us. I summoned the gulls to open the wall because I thought he might be bringing news about Silvester . . .'

Faith's voice trailed away. Rixon could tell what she was thinking: Rixon had indeed brought news about Silvester, news that he was dead. And at least one person on the island clearly would not accept it.

'Why are you telling him all our secrets?' Thorn demanded. He'd arrived just in time to overhear the end of the conversation.

'Oh, Thorn, you can stand down from your post now . . .' Faith said.

'I know,' Thorn replied, throwing down the spears he'd been carrying, 'and I also know what

Rixon is. He's a spy.'

Thorn pointed one threatening finger and marched away again. Rixon heard Rose ask Faith what a spy was, and he heard Faith reply, pretending she knew. Thorn, meanwhile, began striding around the beach apparently searching for something very specific—rocks, big ones.

'So is a spy a kind of birdwatcher? Like the secret society?' Rose said to Faith.

'Hang on,' Rixon interrupted before Faith could reply, 'what "society", Rose?' He was thinking of the will; specifically the part which had left all of Silvester's money to some strange group of local seagull enthusiasts.

'I was too young, but Faith remembers them . . .' Rose began hesitantly.

'They are Silvester's friends,' Faith said quickly. She seemed reluctant to add much more but equally keen to display her knowledge. 'I had to hide when they came; we all did,' Faith continued, 'but Silvester explained it . . . They love seagulls. And these are very special ones on the island. Nobody must disturb them. So Silvester said, if they built the curtains, the wall, then these would hide the seagulls.'

'But they would also hide *you* . . .' Rixon said.

'Why?'

Rose half opened her mouth to speak before Faith urgently shook her head. 'Don't,' Faith instructed.

Rixon needed an answer. He would have persisted. But at that moment, Thorn took over.

'Look, look at me!'

Thorn's voice came from the sea, from the lagoon of water which lay between the shore of the island and the curtain. Thorn was standing in it, waist deep, and above his head, in two hands, he was holding the prize he'd been seeking on the beach. It was a huge rock, almost the size of a small suitcase but pointed at one end.

The fact that Thorn was even able to lift something that big amazed Rixon, but what truly horrified him was the prospect of what Thorn was going to do with it. For Thorn was standing alongside the boat, the ferry that Rixon had hijacked and then left to drift, forgotten, once he'd come ashore.

'No!' Rixon yelled.

"Thorn, you idiot, don't . . . !' Rose shouted, desperately.

But if Thorn heard either of these voices, he paid them no attention.

The crash was enormous. Thorn did not simply release the rock; he actually threw it, using every ounce of his strength to slam it down on the boat beneath him.

Rixon had no way of knowing how big the hole was in the floor of the boat. But he knew it was there. He knew it because the boat was sinking; he knew it because Thorn was grinning.

'No!' Rixon yelled again. He tried to run. He knew he had to get to the boat, to do something, anything. But he couldn't move. Faith's arms held his shoulders, Rose's hand pushed back his chest.

'It's too late,' Faith told him.

'He's too strong,' Rose told him.

Thorn was just laughing.

'Look—' Thorn gestured proudly towards the boat, the stern now almost completely submerged '—how is the spy going to tell anyone our secrets now, eh? How is he going to tell the people who sent him? Rose, I'm protecting us, from him!'

Thorn pointed at Rixon, seawater dripping from the muscles of his forearm, his teeth glinting in a sneer.

'Protecting us?' Rose shouted back. 'From

Rixon? Thorn, you've just invited him to live with us.'

'What?' Thorn replied, a frown suddenly breaking across his face, his arm dropping by his side. 'What do you mean?'

But if he didn't understand Rose's words then Rixon did, perfectly. Both the girls were still restraining him but really there was no need—Rixon no longer possessed the strength to walk, let alone fight. His limbs and his heart were hollow. His eyes were fixed on the bubbles that raced to the surface of the water as the sea consumed his boat.

'What she means,' Rixon said slowly, 'is that I can't leave Splinter Island.'

Chapter 5

Rixon divided his thoughts into two: what he had and what he didn't have. The second part was such a long and horrible list, Rixon felt sick by the time he got to the end of it.

He didn't have a boat, he didn't have a phone which worked, he didn't have any idea if his mum knew where he was; in fact, he didn't have any idea if anyone in the world knew where he was. After all, Splinter Island officially didn't even exist.

What he did have was a rucksack.

He'd made his packed lunch that morning, a lifetime ago. He pulled the old ice-cream tub out of the bag just to have something to hold which reminded him of home, something familiar. Rixon had no appetite. But the children of Splinter Island certainly did.

Thorn had stomped off, his clothes soaked and his face thunderous. But the others now swarmed around Rixon on the beach. Even Russell had joined them from his secret hiding place.

'Oh, my goodness,' Rose exclaimed, 'that looks like cheese. Is that really cheese?'

'Well, yes,' Rixon confirmed, 'just sliced brown bread and cheddar . . .'

'Cheddar . . .' Rose breathed the word like it was a magic spell as she gently took the sandwich. 'When was the last time we had cheese, Russell?'

The boy in the baseball cap immediately raised three fingers of his left hand.

'Three days ago?' Rixon suggested.

'Three years ago,' Russell replied.

'Cheese has an excess of fats and is completely unsuitable,' Faith quickly said. 'Silvester explained that to us many times.'

Rixon noticed that it didn't stop Faith taking a bite of the sandwich as soon as Rose had gleefully completed her mouthful. The remains were then passed to Russell.

'So, what do you eat then?' Rixon asked.

'A perfectly balanced combination of vegetables, pulses, and fruits,' Faith answered.

'We grow those—some of them—on our farm,'

Rose added.

'In addition, we have the special supplies that Silvester brings whenever he goes on a trip,' Faith continued.

'He's always come home . . . before . . .' Rose said, her voice trailing away and her eyes briefly fixing on Faith.

'Are you allowed to eat biscuits?' Rixon reached into the rucksack. He'd brought a whole packet with him.

'Oh, my day of days,' Rose purred. 'Is that chocolate? Do they have actual chocolate on them?'

They actually did. Rose ripped open the packaging and distributed the biscuits between them. Faith took two extra. 'For Thorn,' she explained.

If they hadn't had cheese for three years, Rixon could only guess at the last time any of them had consumed chocolate. It seemed like a cruel existence. But then he thought about Thorn's immense strength, Faith's height, Rose's agility. These were not weaklings; far from it. Only Russell, his eyes still hidden behind sunglasses, seemed skinny. The things they said they ate here were, after all, exactly the things everyone said you were supposed to eat.

The things your parents told you to eat.

If there were other adults on Splinter Island, there was no trace of them. The children certainly hadn't referred to anyone else, apart from the saintly Silvester. There was one question so bold and big in Rixon's mind he now simply had to ask it.

'What are you doing here?' Rixon said.

The munching of biscuits and the licking of fingers suddenly ceased. Rose looked at Faith, Russell looked at Faith, Faith looked at Rixon. Her stare felt like a test. So he stared right back.

'OK, let's go,' Faith said eventually.

'Where to?' Rixon replied, suddenly wondering if there was another part of the island, a jetty where other boats were stored and maybe even a phone?

'To the museum,' Faith answered.

'A museum?' Rixon exclaimed. Out of all the things he was hoping to find on the island, a museum seemed the most preposterous. But the children were serious.

Faith turned to Russell and, to Rixon's surprise, seemed to be asking him for permission. 'Is that OK?'

Russell hesitated for a second and then nodded.

So they went, Russell leading the way through

a narrow gap between two small silver birch trees and into another small clearing which, Rose proudly declared, was the farm.

To Rixon, it looked more like a big vegetable patch. It was clear from the dug-over earth and canes stuck in the ground that many things had been growing here, in the past. It was equally clear that very little was growing now.

'There are some potatoes, on the way . . .' Rose said, pointing to a few green leaves sprouting from piles of earthy dust. 'It's not been a good year, so far,' she admitted.

'Yes, and that's why Silvester went to fetch the irritation system,' Faith declared.

'Irrigation,' Russell immediately corrected. 'We need to distribute our rainwater more efficiently. Silvester left for the mainland to buy a new irrigation system sixty-three days ago . . .'

'Yes, well, let's not worry about that now,' Faith said briskly. 'We're wasting our time here.'

Rixon had brought news of Silvester's death; Faith, he noticed, was clearly struggling to accept he was gone for good.

Just as the 'farm' had turned out to be a patch of dry earth, the 'museum' turned out to be a rickety old shed. Its walls were planks of brown wood turning green with moss. The roof sloped from left to right and was covered in threadbare grey felt.

Leaning up against one side of the hut was a long metal pole which looked as if it was keeping the whole structure upright. It was like a piece of scaffolding embedded in the ground at one end and propping up the hut with the other.

'It was supposed to make electricity,' Rose said, following Rixon's eyes.

'That piece of metal?'

'It didn't work. Silvester was very disappointed at first but then he said it didn't matter. He said it was for the best.'

'Rose, what do you mean?'

'Come on, Russell has opened the museum!' Faith's voice cut through their conversation.

Russell was standing at the threshold of the hut, the door open behind him.

'You noticed the wind turbine, Rixon?' he said.

'Wind turbine, of course, that's what it is . . .' Rixon had seen loads of them before, naturally, but normally they were much bigger. And normally they stood upright in fields rather than propping up old sheds.

'How did it get here?' Rixon asked.

But Russell didn't answer. He'd disappeared into the gloom of the 'museum' and all Rixon could do was follow.

It took Rixon's eyes several seconds to adjust to the darkness, and even then there was nothing for them to focus on, nothing that looked like it belonged in a museum, anyway.

There was just a big table, and slumped on top was a heap of old plastic. But Russell stood alongside it with his hands clasped behind his back as if he was studying a precious religious relic. It was only when Rixon looked again that it reminded him of something.

Searching his memory, he was taken back to the previous summer. One Saturday afternoon, he'd gone to the local pool for a friend's swimming party. It wasn't a normal session—they'd put out the 'inflatables'. The procedure was to sprint and jump from the side of the pool onto a plastic platform supported by inflatable tubes. Then you fell off. It was fun.

What lay in front of him now was a grubby, saggy version of that inflatable platform. It was patched up with sticky tape in several places as it slouched on the table. But it looked big enough to sit in.

'Is that a raft?' Rixon said with a sudden burst of inspiration.

'Yes,' answered Russell, 'of course it is.'

'But why is it here? Why do you keep it?' To Rixon's eyes it just looked like rubbish.

'We keep it because it reminds us of the day we were saved,' Faith's voice boomed from the doorway of the shed, 'by the greatest man in the world.'

'Your relation, Rixon,' Rose said, alongside her, 'Silvester.'

'You see, that's where we were,' Russell said, motioning his hands towards the raft, 'when Silvester saved us.'

Rixon looked at each of them in turn and then back at the raft. Was it possible?

'Thorn too?' he said, 'All of you on there?'

Faith nodded, 'We were smaller, of course.'

'Russell was six, me and Thorn were seven, Faith was eight, when it . . . happened,' Rose said.

'We celebrate it every year, the day we were rescued,' Russell added.

'Which day is that?' Rixon asked.

The children just shrugged.

'Silvester tells us,' Rose said, 'but we know it's near the start of the summer because it's always a night when the sun begins to win the fight against the darkness . . .'

'We have had five celebrations on Splinter Island,' Russell said, answering a question that Rixon had just been preparing to ask.

Five celebrations—the children had been on this island for five years. Rixon turned it over in his mind. It seemed impossible, however he tried to process it.

'But how many times have you been back, you know, home?' he asked.

Rose and Faith just looked back at him blankly.

'Never, of course,' Faith answered.

'This is home,' Rose said. 'Silvester told us, Splinter Island is our home.'

'Silvester . . . but hang on,' Rixon said, still desperately trying to fit it all together. 'You mean, Silvester trapped you here?'

'Trapped? Oh no, Rixon, not trapped—you cannot say that, you must not,' Russell insisted, his voice suddenly filled with passion. 'He saved us, Rixon, saved us.'

'Yes,' Faith said, 'we had no one, after our parents had gone . . .' Faith still stood tall. In the frame of the doorway, she was like a pillar, arms folded, legs shoulder-width apart. But however strong she made herself appear, Faith could not hide the sadness in her voice. 'They told us it was an adventure, a midnight holiday . . .'

'Who did?'

'Our parents, Rixon . . .'

'Oh, so they were with you? You were all together? On the raft?'

'We weren't on the raft, of course we weren't; not at the start. They hired a boat, a big one, big enough to carry the wind turbine and everything else. It had beds at the back, you know, underneath. We were all asleep on the boat when it happened—' Faith paused for a second '—but we woke up when we heard the bang . . .'

'There was an explosion?' Rixon asked.

'There was a bomb,' Faith replied.

'What?!'

'That's what Faith thinks, Rixon,' Rose said, picking her words carefully. 'About the bomb, I mean. I don't know, maybe the boat could have hit some rocks . . .'

'Rose, the boat was smashed up; it was in pieces,' Faith insisted.

'I know Faith, I know.'

'And your parents?' Rixon said, as gently as he could.

Faith just shook her head. 'They were up at

the other end, trying to navigate. We shouted for them, but it was dark. And the rain was pouring, so hard. We were soaking, the boat was sinking. All we could find was the life raft. Russell grabbed a suitcase . . .' Faith said.

'It felt like hours that we were drifting there. It was so frightening, so frightening . . .'—Rose was almost whispering now—'we didn't think anybody would come.'

'But hang on, hang on, stop,' Rixon insisted, his mind racing, trying to keep up with the story. It seemed so horrible, so crazy. 'But why? I mean, why were you in the boat? Where were you going?'

'To Splinter Island, of course,' Faith replied.

'Your parents, they knew Splinter Island was here, that it existed?' Rixon asked in fresh amazement.

'My mother was a geologist,' Faith explained. 'She'd studied details of discoveries going back centuries, places where they found rare rocks and minerals, places the world had forgotten about, Rixon.'

'And they wanted to bring you here?'

'To escape from the bad people,' Rose said darkly.

'To complete the work,' Russell added.

'Complete? What work? What bad people?'

'That doesn't matter, Rixon,' Faith declared, the tone of control returning. 'All we know is that we were safe here, we are safe here. Silvester told us that.'

'He heard us, you see,' Rose said. 'He was on the island—it was his special place, his secret place but he heard the explosion and he came to rescue us. Even though it was a few miles away, in the dark and the storm, he came.'

'But why,' Rixon tried again, 'why didn't he just take you home?'

'Oh, Rixon, think about it.' Russell said sharply and turned to face Rixon directly. 'If they'd tried to blow us up once, surely they were going to try it again?'

Rixon was silent then. It wasn't that he didn't have any more questions; in fact, he had too many. But the Splinter Islanders closed ranks. They joined together in a huddle at the entrance to the museum, arms around each other's shoulders. Rose, Rixon heard, was sniffing back tears. But Faith was taking charge.

'That's enough,' she said, 'we've said all we need to. We have to keep going, we have to stay strong, we have to live.'

'We have to eat,' Russell said.

'Yes, Russell, you're right, and that reminds me . . . come on.'

Half pushing, half leading, Faith encouraged the others back into the open air. After one more look at the remains of the raft on the 'museum' table, Rixon followed. He felt both entranced and excluded by these people. Their story was so extraordinary he'd almost forgotten his own.

When he caught up with them, they were standing beneath a particularly tall pine tree. Its trunk split into two different directions, making it look like a capital 'Y'. Faith and Rose were already in the midst of an animated discussion.

'But should we? Is it right?' Rose said.

'Rose, do we have a choice? We need to eat,' Faith replied.

'I know, but Silvester always says—I mean, said—that they're our friends. The birds are our friends, even pigeons.'

'Yes, Rose, but he also says that in an emergency, we should do whatever we can to survive.'

'Yes, but—'

'And how much is there, you know, left?'

Rose didn't speak but Rixon saw her shrug.

'Exactly,' said Faith. 'It's an emergency and a new pigeon nest means fresh eggs. So it's decided.'

With a gentle nod, Rose made up her mind. She sprinted forward towards the trunk of the tree, sprang into the air, and grabbed onto a branch a metre above her head.

Without pausing, she pulled herself up onto the branch and jumped again, arms outstretched, to grab the one above.

'Quick, Rose, quick . . . before the birds come back,' Faith implored her from below.

By now, Rose was halfway up. Rixon stood watching, transfixed by her strength and agility.

That was his mistake.

One second, Rixon was standing upright, wondering if Rose was really going to make it all the way to the top and grab the eggs. The next second, he was flying, with every breath of air suddenly squeezed from his lungs. He'd been hit, straight in the chest, by a runaway train. That was all he could think of as everything turned to darkness.

Chapter 6

Rixon could see nothing, but he knew he was alive. He knew that for certain because he could feel pain in the pit of his stomach. For a split second, the pain eased as he sensed himself rise, and then he gasped as he fell again, hard.

He was being carried . . . somewhere.

The motion was bumpy but the rhythm was slowing to a walking pace. Rixon felt arms gripping his legs tightly. He could hear deep breaths in his ear growing longer as the pace grew slower until the movement finally stopped.

Now Rixon remembered what his dad had called it. He could even remember what it had felt like, although it had been so many years ago.

He was being held in a fireman's lift.

His body was balanced over someone's shoulder with his head hanging forwards, face down, over the carrier's back. But what made Rixon panic was the hood. He could not see because his head was covered. He could taste the fabric of a sack on his lips as the string tightened around his neck.

His throat stung as he tried to gulp for air but instead inhaled sharp shards of the sack's strands. He lashed out with his free hands, punching at the back which supported him. At the same time, with as much force as he could summon up, Rixon kicked his legs free from the arms which had held him.

Rixon was aware of only one other thing before he fell.

He suddenly heard the sound of a great wave crashing as his head hit the ground like a pebble being thrown onto the shore. Then he felt nothing.

As Rixon's senses slowly returned he imagined he was cast adrift on a furious ocean, consumed by fog. He could not see his own hands, he could not feel his own feet. The pain in his stomach was only bearable when he fixed his concentration on the throbbing in his head instead. He was nowhere. He was floating. He was lying on a rock.

Splarrr! Rixon yelled, spitting out a mouthful

of watery blood.

He could feel cold stone beneath his cheek. The right side of his torso was soaking wet but his legs were still numb.

'Why am I lying down?' Rixon asked himself as he tried to remember how to move. Slowly he forced his brain into gear. He'd been struck, he'd been carried, he'd been . . .

'The sack!'

If he could shout, he knew one thing; the hood that had cloaked him had gone. Someone must have removed it because Rixon had no recollection of doing it himself.

But if the sack had been removed, why was his world black?

When Rixon turned his head upwards, he could see no sky; he couldn't see anything. And there was something else missing too; there was no wind, not even a breeze. Rixon closed his eyes and opened them again, trying to force them to work. He rubbed his eyes with his fingers and immediately wished he hadn't, for they stung viciously.

'Owww, why?' he groaned to himself.

Slowly Rixon brought the fingers of his right hand to his lips. They were wet but there was something else—salt. If the mists inside his mind had cleared, if he was conscious and not dreaming, then Rixon believed he was lying in a pool of seawater.

It was then that he heard the waves.

They were close enough to make Rixon think he was lying on a beach. But how could he be when he was surrounded by darkness? Rixon felt as though he was stuck in a stone box.

Or a cave.

'A cave!'

When Rixon shouted these words, the echo he heard in return confirmed it. And if he was in a cave, then Rixon knew one thing for certain: he wanted to get out. But when he tried to haul himself to his feet, he almost fell. There was water all around his ankles, resisting his steps. Instead of walking, he had to paddle.

He stretched his arms out to help his balance, and his palms felt rock, dry rock. But his legs were getting wetter all the time. Within half a dozen steps, the water level was at his knees.

Still Rixon's head ached, and his mind whirled. But he had to think. The sea, he knew, moved. There were tides. And if the tide was coming in, then the cave was filling up.

Rixon's instinct was to retreat from the waves he felt coming towards him. But when he turned, he could only feel a wall of rock behind him. There was simply nowhere to go. He had to press on into the darkness ahead of him, fighting the tide of water, fighting the tide of panic. He was fighting time in a desperate race to escape.

Rixon's heart leapt as he saw something ahead of him. It was a little circle of light in the distance. Could it be sunlight? It was something to hope for . . . something to swim for. The water was now up to his waist.

Rixon could sense the light getting brighter ahead but the ceiling of rock was sloping downwards so low that the water filled the entire space in front of him.

There was nothing else for Rixon to do but throw himself forward, hold his breath, and hope.

It took him a dozen strokes.

A dozen times Rixon scraped his hands on the sides of the cave wall, a dozen times he banged his head. It was like trying to swim through a tunnel without knowing when or where it would end.

The sound that told Rixon he was free was the roar of the open sea. The thirteenth breaststroke took him out of the cave . . . and straight into trouble.

Rixon's overwhelming sense of relief was replaced instantly by fear. He was exhausted; his clothes felt like weights dragging him downwards; and in front of him now was a wall of waves.

This side of the island was savage. Rixon could just make out the line of huge curtains concealing the island from the outside world. But it didn't keep out the waves. In fact, it seemed to intensify their ferocity. There was no beach here, just a cliff face; and the sea was crashing and rebounding against it. Rixon was using every drop of his remaining energy to strain against the waves, to stop himself being thrown against the rocks like a pebble.

Going back was not an option, Rixon knew that. Only the cave lay behind him and that would be filled up with water now. He held on to a small ledge of rock and braced himself with his feet against the cliff wall beneath the surface. Straining to see, Rixon thought he could make out a patch of sand to his left where the sea seemed to be coming to shore far more calmly. Could he possibly get there? Could he really swim that far?

Rixon didn't have a choice. A sudden wave,

stronger than any that had come before, tore Rixon away from the cliff wall and flung him into the open water. He gulped a mouthful of seawater and then another. Rixon's throat burned with salt, his arms thrashed, but his body tensed in panic as his feet reached for the seabed and couldn't find it.

Too deep.

Rixon stretched every muscle in his neck to keep his head above water when—*boom!*—another wave caught him just as he opened his mouth for air. Rixon swallowed a lungful of ice cold seawater. He felt the fight in his limbs suddenly fade. He saw the beams of light from the sun flicker and play on the sea in front of him and then he just felt himself sink. The water was like a sea monster with a thousand arms pulling him towards the bed of the ocean, and Rixon was now powerless to resist.

He was just another victim at the mercy of the sea.

He let himself be carried.

But the only direction was down.

Until the arm grabbed him.

'Thorn, you idiot!'

'What have you done? Is he dead? Is Rixon dead?'

'Of course he's not dead. Look at him, he's fine …'

'He's not fine, he's just lying there …'

'I saw you, Thorn, from the top of the tree. I saw you put a sack over his head and run off with him.'

'We've been looking for you everywhere!'

Rixon heard Rose, Faith, and Thorn talking, but he didn't have the strength to join in their conversation. He was lying flat on the ground, soaking wet and exhausted.

'I was waiting for him. I knew he'd come out. I was lying on the rock—you know the place, just where the cave opens out to the sea,' Thorn said defensively. 'I grabbed him, didn't I? I carried him up here to be safe, didn't I?'

'But why did you put him in there, Thorn?' Rose screamed back. 'You know that cave fills up at high tide, we all do. You took him and you left him. You left him to drown!'

'I wasn't going to hurt him. I rescued him didn't I? I just wanted to test him.'

'Test him? By drowning him?' Rose raged at her brother.

Faith was calmer, but only slightly. 'Thorn, you

know Silvester says that cave is out of bounds.'

'Yes, he ruled it as too dangerous.' This confirmation came from Russell, who had now joined the group.

'Well, maybe *he* can decide what's dangerous now. Why don't you ask him—he owns the place now, doesn't he?' Thorn snapped with an accusing finger pointed straight at Rixon. 'Anyway, it's only a cave. Anyone can get out of a cave,' he added contemptuously.

Rixon saw the children turn to look at him. Slowly he began pushing himself up into a sitting position. The skin on his palms felt raw and he winced. From his fingers to his toes, every part of him was in pain. But a new energy was starting to surge through his body, a force rising inside him, like the lava inside a volcano before its eruption. Rixon Webster was furious.

'It's difficult to get out of a cave,' he spat out, looking at Thorn, 'when it's filling up with water, while you are lying unconscious.'

Rixon rose to his feet and gave himself a second to steady himself. He allowed himself a look around. In front of him were the children; behind them was the edge of the cliff; and below that, some ten metres down, was the sea. That was all Rixon needed to know. Then he charged at Thorn.

He bent at the waist and, like a bull, snorting and steaming, rammed his shoulder just beneath Thorn's ribcage.

'Hey . . . !' Thorn gasped. He was more shocked than hurt, and it was that element of surprise which swung things in Rixon's favour.

'Rixon, no!' Rose shouted, but if Rixon heard, he ignored her.

Rixon now wrapped his right arm around Thorn's legs so that, just for a second, he was actually carrying him, pushing him forward.

'Rixon, the cliff!' It was Faith's voice this time, close to him. But that didn't stop Rixon. The only thing that halted him was Thorn's knee, catching Rixon in the stomach as he slipped backwards beneath him. The bull stumbled and fell.

When Rixon looked down, he could see two things. First, he saw Thorn's face in a panicked grimace just below his own nose. Second, directly below Thorn's head, Rixon saw the sea.

Rixon was lying on top of Thorn, still gripping his shoulders, both boys perched right on the cliff edge. Their heads and necks were actually hanging over the void. One more metre, one more split second of the raging bull, and they would both have toppled right off.

'OK, OK,' Thorn's voice came, weak and desperate, his eyes flashing with fear. 'OK, Rixon, you win.'

Rixon felt Thorn weaken beneath him. The anger had swept through his own body like a gale. Now the fury had passed, Rixon needed a strong hand to pull him backwards, to help him to his feet.

'Careful now,' Faith said. 'That was so dangerous—you both could have been killed.' Faith sounded cross, but there was also a note of awe in her voice. Rixon had demonstrated a hidden strength, that was certain.

As Thorn scrambled to his feet, his sister strode up to him and punched his arm hard, just below his shoulder.

'Thorn, you are an idiot,' Rose said. Then she turned towards Rixon. 'Rixon, you are an idiot too,' Rose said. She didn't punch him but her hand was shaking.

Faith moved behind Rose and gently placed her long right arm around her shoulders, first holding her back in restraint and then softening into an embrace. Rose turned her head onto

Faith's chest. Faith stroked Rose's long, unruly hair with her right hand and beckoned Russell over with her left.

'Russell, can you remind everyone here of Silvester's second golden rule?'

Russell nodded, held up his right hand with his first two fingers outstretched, and said, 'Golden rule number two: the children of Splinter Island must love, respect, and care for each other at all times.'

Faith nodded. 'Yes, thank you, Russell,' she said, and pointed at Thorn. 'Thorn, you have clearly and totally broken Silvester's second golden rule.'

'No, no, I haven't!' Thorn insisted, straightening himself up. 'I haven't broken the rule because he isn't—' Thorn flung an arm in the direction of Rixon.

'Isn't what?' Faith said.

'—he isn't one of the children of Splinter Island. He isn't one of us. Can't you see that? Silvester wrote those rules for *us*. He did everything for *us*. He protected us and fed us; he *saved* us. Now this boy turns up and he's trying to riddle us. He wants to take over. He comes here and says he owns us. He is *not* a child of Splinter Island,'

Thorn finished by punching his open palm with his fist.

'Well, I say he is.' Rose was not resting on Faith any more. She was standing upright, and she was forthright. 'This is Silvester's family, Thorn, right here. Silvester's family. Him. Rixon, Rixon Webster.' Now Rose was pointing at Rixon. He felt as if he was on display, like a toddler caught between bickering parents. He might have overpowered Thorn once, but he knew that, as a group, the children would always be stronger than him. He needed their approval; that was vital.

'I am going to be honest with you,' Rixon said, taking a deep breath. 'In my whole life, I have never, ever even met Silvester.'

'Hah!' Thorn roared. 'That proves it! That proves he's a riddler, he's a liar!'

'Of course it doesn't, Thorn,' Faith replied calmly. 'How could Rixon have met Silvester? He's spent the last five years on this island looking after us, almost every day he's been right here.'

That was just the point, the part of it which still made no sense to Rixon.

'Why did Silvester keep you here?' he asked, trying to keep his voice as neutral as he could. 'Why didn't he just take you home? I know your parents . . .' He hesitated.

'They are dead, yes, Rixon,' Faith said simply.

'OK,' Rixon continued, 'but what was Silvester protecting you from? What was the danger?'

There was no answer. Faith, Rose, and even Thorn all just turned their eyes to look at one person: Russell.

He sighed, made a small adjustment to the sunglasses over his eyes, and said, 'It's all because of the box. The special box, the one that was going to save the world.'

Chapter 7

The only thing that Rixon wanted to talk about was the 'special box'. Whatever it was, Rixon felt certain it had to be the key to everything. After all, Russell had said it was going to save the world! But, infuriatingly, nobody would say another word about it. If there was a secret it was staying that way. The lid was firmly closed.

'There's no time for that,' Faith insisted. 'It will be dark soon. No more questions.'

Thorn had, to Rixon's relief, stomped away in a huff as soon as the clifftop confrontation was over. But the other Splinter Islanders were busying themselves in the clearing where, Rixon gathered, dinner of some description would be served. Rixon also discovered there was far more to the trees than met the eye.

'It's a cupboard,' Faith explained, pointing.

'It's a tree trunk,' Rixon replied, staring.

Faith beamed, grabbed a small knot in the wood and pulled. To Rixon's amazement a curved door opened in her hand. Part of the trunk had been hollowed out to create a secret hiding place. There were small hinges inside, but the bark of the tree remained entirely intact, so it was almost impossible to tell the door was actually there.

'We have one each,' Faith explained. 'Nobody is allowed to open another person's tree cupboard.'

'Is that one of Silvester's golden rules?'

'No Rixon, it's one of mine,' Faith said, reaching into the tree trunk and pulling out something which revealed itself to be a shirt, 'and this is one of my spares. It's a lot drier than what you're wearing now. There are some shorts here too, they should fit.'

Rixon smiled; to be offered clothes by Faith was, he hoped, a new sign of respect. More to the point he was still soaked to the skin, his jeans were so heavy after his immersion in the sea they felt like metal chains tied to his legs.

The shirt he now pulled on was striped blue and white. It was, he noticed, almost identical to the one Faith herself was wearing.

'I've got hundreds of them. Well, a lot, anyway,'

Faith explained. 'Silvester wears them too; he buys them when he goes on his trips.'

Faith closed her cupboard door and left Rixon to finished getting changed. But he wasn't alone for long.

'Rixon, come and look at this, quick.' Rose beckoned him from the trunk of another birch tree. Rixon couldn't tell if her own secret cupboard was located there but he could see that Rose was holding something, her left hand was clasped shut.

'Your fingers,' she whispered, as Rixon approached. 'Let me see them.'

Rixon had been trying hard to ignore the intense pain in his hands but, in fact, his fingers were so sore he'd barely been able to button up his new shirt. He'd grazed his knuckles horribly on the cave wall and then cut his fingertips on the rocks he'd grabbed, desperately fighting the power of the sea.

'Don't worry,' said Rose. 'This normally works.'

Now Rose slowly opened her left hand. As her fingers straightened, Rixon saw something extraordinary in her palm. It was beautiful. Its intricate blue surface resembled dozens of tiny, glass staircases running into each other, all glinting in the sunlight.

'It's a crystal,' Rose explained, her voice still hushed. 'There are lots of them on the island, or underneath it, really. You can find them in the caves, but Silvester says it's too dangerous. I mean, he said. Well, anyway . . . he let me keep this one.'

'But what is it? I mean, does it have a name?' Rixon asked, to his eyes it looked like a blue diamond.

Rose shrugged. 'I think it's "cobbled", maybe because it's sort of bumpy? But, look, it works. You just have to believe in it.' Gently she held the crystal over the knuckles of Rixon's right hand where the worst cuts were. 'Just believe in it . . .' Rose whispered again and she slowly passed the crystal back and forth so it lightly brushed Rixon's skin.

Amazingly, almost immediately, he felt better. At first the skin on his hand felt cold as if someone had placed an ice cube there, but then it started to tingle. When Rixon looked at his fingers, he really thought that some of the cuts had started to heal, and the pain . . . it was clearing. Whether it was down to his mind or his body, it was working.

Rose smiled at him. 'I told you,' she said.

Rixon then had a dozen questions ready to ask, but Faith was calling their names. Faith wanted to organize the evening meal and Rose was anxious to comply.

They soon had their instructions. Russell was to make a fire in the clearing while Rose and Rixon were to proceed directly to what Faith referred to as 'the store'.

'It isn't far,' Rose said, 'this way.'

Rixon, jogging to keep up, followed her along another winding path almost overgrown with wild vegetation. Rose seemed to know her way instinctively. She pressed on ahead, but this was Rixon's chance.

'Rose!' he called to her, 'wait a minute, I need to ask you, the special box, you must . . .'

'I've told you Rixon,' she snapped back, half turning to face him, 'I don't know anything about that.'

'But Russell said . . .'

'I don't know anything about what Russell said.'

'Oh, so what do you know then?' Rixon demanded, infuriated. He sprinted forward, ahead of Rose, and then pivoted suddenly to confront her, to stop her in her tracks. 'I mean, do you ever even go to school?' he exclaimed.

Rose halted, folded her arms and replied calmly, 'I'm perfectly capable of reading and writing, if that's what you mean. I knew all the words I needed before we left the mainland. Well, a lot of them. The rest of them Silvester taught us.'

'Oh, Silvester taught you?' Rixon said, motioning with his hands and slowly turning his head, 'But where? Am I missing something? I can't actually see a school anywhere.'

'You think you learn everything sitting indoors, Rixon?' Rose enquired.

'Well, I don't know how else—' Rixon began to answer.

'In the summer, we do tree-climbing and sea-swimming, but there are so many things to study on the island. Look, what's that?' Rose said, pointing to a tall tree immediately behind Rixon.

He turned to examine it. 'Well, it's a tree,' Rixon eventually replied.

'Ha! Is that a joke? Of course it's a tree. What *type* of tree is it?'

Rixon turned to look again. It was tall and mostly green, with little spiky bits like needles coating the branches. It was wide at the bottom and grew to a point at the top.

'I'd say it's a Christmas tree,' Rixon said. 'A massive Christmas tree.'

'It's a Norfolk Island pine,' Rose said with a withering look in his direction. 'It is not indigenous to this part of the world, therefore . . . ?' She waited for Rixon to follow her train of thought; he couldn't.

'Well, come on, Rixon. It means someone planted them. It is a sign that people were here a long time ago. Maybe they planted them for logging; maybe they wanted to make their own furniture or their own log cabins.'

'Oh, right . . .' Rixon mumbled. 'Um, who were these people, actually?'

'Miners, I think. Someone had to dig up the crystal—well, that's my theory. Silvester always says we have to learn to think for ourselves. Don't they tell you that at your school?'

He didn't know what to say. Rixon hadn't been taught how to answer that.

'Quick,' Rose hissed, her voice suddenly dropping to a whisper, 'turn around slowly—no, the other way—quietly now. It's resting on that long branch.'

'What, Rose; what am I looking at?' Rixon whispered back.

'The bird of course, the yellow bird . . .'

Rixon saw it now and he even knew what it was. His grandma used to have one. Although she kept hers in the living room, in a cage.

'It's a canary!' Rixon exclaimed, startling the little bird away, 'Oh, sorry . . . but why, I mean, what is a canary doing here?'

'The miners brought them, I think. When they were digging up the blue minerals, the crystals. The birds settled here and bred. They lasted a lot longer than the miners. But I mean it's obvious why they'd want canaries, isn't it?'

Rixon could only shake his head.

'They smelled gas underground; they were the warning system. If the canaries died, then the miners knew they had to get out quickly. But it didn't always work.'

'Oh?'

'Well, when Silvester first came to the island, he said he found four skeletons.'

'Ugh, that's horrible—where?' Rixon asked.

'Oh,'—Rose suddenly seemed hesitant— 'actually they were underground. In exactly the spot where Thorn left you today.'

In exactly the spot where Thorn had left him to become another skeleton, Rixon thought.

'This is a dangerous place,' Rixon muttered.

'Oh, you think so?' Rose answered, sounding genuinely surprised.

'Well, yes, of course it is. I mean, it's basically a wilderness.'

Rose paused for a second. 'Rixon, can I ask you a question?' she said.

'Sure, OK. As long as it's not about trees . . .'

'No, it's about roads. Do you know how many people in the world die on roads each year?'

'Well, no . . .' Rixon confessed.

'1.24 million,' Rose told him. 'Silvester told us that. I wonder why they didn't tell you at your school? With so many people dying, it seems like a useful thing to know about. Oh, and do you know how many people die every year on the roads on Splinter Island?'

Rixon just shrugged.

'I will tell you: zero. Because we don't have any roads on Splinter Island. Now, come on, we're running late.'

With a quick smile, Rose was gone. Rixon stumbled after her.

The store turned out to be a trapdoor. At least,

that's all that was visible at ground level. Rose bent down to creak it open.

'Silvester was going to buy oil, as well, for those hinges,' she muttered before plunging into the depths. It took a few seconds for Rixon to follow; by then, Rose was standing at the foot of a ladder holding a torch to show him the way.

'It's a wind-up one. We keep it here, just for the storeroom,' Rose explained.

Rose shone the torch in an arc to illuminate each corner of what Rixon could now see was a form of cellar.

'This underground room was here when we arrived,' Rose said, 'probably left by the miners and the start of a tunnel they never finished. But we adapted it.'

Rixon could see piles of clothes, thick coats, and woollen hats, ready for the winter, he presumed. There were about a dozen spears and lots of tools too: spades, garden forks, and smaller trowels, all leaning against one wall. But mainly what Rixon could see was shelves.

There were shelves attached to the walls, shelves suspended from the ceiling, shelves piled up on other shelves in the middle of the room. And they all had one thing in common.

They were empty.

'Over here, Rixon; you can choose.' Rose had walked to the far corner of the store and was shining her torch on a small pyramid of tin cans. 'Peas or beans, Rixon; what do you like?'

'Oh, either is fine . . .' he mumbled in reply. Rixon was thinking, he was calculating. He couldn't tell exactly how many tins were piled up but there couldn't be more than fifty. How long would those supplies possibly last for all of them on the island?

Rose followed his thoughts. 'Silvester is getting more food,' she said, 'or, he was . . .'

Rose was silent then. They headed back to the others, clutching five tin cans. Rixon was trying to ignore how horribly hungry he suddenly felt. For the first time in his life, there was no fridge to raid, no kitchen cupboard to open, no shop on the corner. But the residents of Splinter Island *never* had those things.

The reality of the situation suddenly became shockingly clear in Rixon's mind; unless someone came to their rescue, they were going to starve on Splinter Island. And who, exactly, was going to come to their rescue?

Chapter 8

Back in the clearing, a table had been arranged. It was an old door balanced on two oil drums—big tin cans which had once contained cooking oil, according to the labels.

Rixon saw immediately that Thorn was back. He'd tucked his long, blonde hair inside the neck of his T-shirt in preparation for the meal. He was baring his teeth in readiness. Rixon tried not to look. Each of the children had a stone or a tree stump to sit on, which they'd moved into position. Rixon noticed that Faith sat at the head of the table, and that opposite her an old wooden crate had been placed on the ground.

Faith stood up and motioned to it as Rixon approached. 'Please, Rixon, sit there.'

This was obviously quite a compliment. Thorn growled in protest but Rixon took his designated place at the table.

Russell, meanwhile, was crouching over the fire. It was a bit like a barbecue; another old oil drum had been cut in half and filled with sticks and roughly chopped branches. On top there was a wire tray like you'd see in an oven or a grill, and on top of that was a saucepan. Into this Russell now carefully poured the contents of the tins. Beans and peas were mixed together, Rixon noticed.

Russell then handed out five plates.

'You've got Silvester's,' Rose remarked.

'Oh, thank you,' Rixon said and looked over towards Thorn, who was glaring at the table.

Lastly, Russell handed each of them a spoon before he poured a small pile of brown splodge onto each plate. Nobody spoke; they just ate. It was delicious.

At home, Rixon would never eat anything without tomato ketchup unless it was noodles, which he would only eat with soy sauce. Suddenly there was no choice about what to eat, but he loved what was on his plate.

To drink, there was a mug of warm water. Russell had heated a kettle on the fire.

'We collect rainwater in a big tub behind the museum,' Faith explained. 'It's healthier if you boil it first. It's very clean.'

Rixon nodded, removing a piece of leaf from his tongue as subtly as he could.

When Russell had collected all the plates and spoons, Faith stood up.

'This has been a very strange day,' she began, 'a very unusual day. A very . . . different day. So now I suggest that we go to bed.'

'Oh, but not yet,' Rose said. 'I thought we could, you know, sing it—'

'But he's not here,' Thorn objected. 'He always starts it.'

'I know, Thorn, that's the whole point. We need to do something to think of him, to remember Silvester . . .'

'You only remember people when they are dead, Rose,' Thorn replied.

That was Rose's point, Rixon knew. But it was equally clear that her brother still couldn't, or wouldn't, accept the fact that Silvester was no longer alive.

There was silence for a while, until Faith clapped her hands. 'Well, I think it's a good idea. It will cheer us up to sing,' she said. 'Now, Thorn, do you have your drum?'

'You know that I don't,' he sighed. 'It broke,

weeks ago.'

'You hit it too hard—you always do,' Rose told him.

'Well, it doesn't matter,' Faith said, 'just use your hands on the table. Now, Russell, exactly how many strings are left on the guitar?'

Silently Russell raised his index finger into the air, just one finger.

'Aha,' Faith said with a sigh. 'OK, that's no good. Looks like it's just you and your bugle, Rose.'

It turned out that Rose kept her musical instrument hanging on a branch of a nearby tree. It was so badly dented and scratched, Rixon wondered if any sound could possibly emerge from it.

In fact, Rose played it rather beautifully. Her tune consisted of four notes rising in a scale but she held the last one before dropping down and repeating the pattern. It was extremely simple but that's why it worked. The notes seemed to echo through the trees like a lonely beast calling from the depths of the woodland.

Unfortunately Rose's music was just the introduction. Then the singing started.

The whole thing was dominated by Faith's booming vocals. She sang loudly and tunelessly as if she was in the crowd at a football match. Thorn beat his hands on the table in a half-hearted rhythm while Rose sort of hummed along. To Rixon's amazement, she seemed to be enjoying it. He knew he wasn't. But at least the words were funny. Although he wasn't sure they were meant to be.

> 'Splinter Island, Splinter Island, we are
> sitting on the sea,
>   All gathered here together, as one big family.
>   Splinter Island, Splinter Island, the home of
> the free,
>   We're as sharp as a spear, we're as strong
> as a tree.'

After repeating each line twice, Faith mercifully stopped.

'Oh yes, very . . . powerful,' Rixon managed to say, delivering a short round of applause.

'Silvester wrote those words himself,' Rose explained.

'It's the anthem of our independence,' Faith added.

'Because of the territorial boundaries,' Russell said. He had taken no active part in the singing apart from crouching near the barbecue and covering his ears.

'What do you mean?' Rixon asked.

'Our distance from the mainland is over twelve nautical miles,' Russell clarified.

'Right, so?'

'So that means, right here, we're in international waters. We're not part of any country or territory.'

'We are independent,' Faith declared proudly.

'That's why Silvester loved it here,' Rose added.

That's why he loved it here. Rixon repeated those words in his mind. Well, who wouldn't love to be free from all the rules and responsibilities? Splinter Island had very few of the things Rixon took for granted in his normal life. Television, the Internet, running water, even electricity; none of those things seemed to be here. But then there was nobody to tell you what to do. Splinter Island was freedom. It was also the perfect place to hide.

The only thing Rixon felt certain about was that he had to get home, but he had no idea how that could possibly happen. The sky above him was starting to turn from brilliant blue to vivid orange. Rixon had begun the day imagining what

Splinter Island might possibly be like without even knowing it existed. Now he was here, at the day's end, knowing it was real; but he still struggled to believe it.

Rixon wanted his bed and he wanted his mum. What he had was Faith, issuing more instructions.

'Come on Rixon, we must get to the sleeping quarters before dark.'

She led him to the tallest tree at the far end of the clearing, to a ladder which was nailed to the trunk and up to a platform. This was, Rixon realized, as he forced his hands onto the final rung, the very place where the children of Splinter Island had stood to throw spears at him.

'Is this where you sleep?' Rixon asked, looking around him for something that might resemble a bed. 'Of course not,' Faith replied. 'Our bedroom is coming,' she added with a smile.

Russell and Rose were already on the platform hunched over a kind of wheel. It looked like the plastic drum Rixon used in the garden to coil the hosepipe around. Watering the plants was his job, and tidying up afterwards was always the hardest bit. He had to force down the handle and hope the hose didn't get tangled. This arrangement looked similar except the empty drum was bigger and made of metal.

'We turn the handle and pull it up,' Rose explained. 'Normally Thorn does it. But—'

'He will be sleeping elsewhere this evening,' Faith quickly interjected.

That was something, Rixon thought. Of all the uncertainties and dangers that lay on Splinter Island, Thorn was the most threatening.

But Rixon still had no idea what Rose was going to 'pull up'.

It took all of her strength to do it. At one point, Russell joined in, his hands interlocking with Rose's on the handle. It turned slowly and creaked repeatedly, but soon Rixon saw a cable, a thick metallic rope, begin to gather around the drum.

'Don't look there, look down!' Faith instructed Rixon as she too grabbed part of the handle and forced it through another revolution.

Rixon turned his eyes towards the forest floor. He could see a big pile of chopped wood and branches. Except it couldn't be a pile because it was moving. Or rather, something was moving *inside* it. Something was rising, something that was attached to the cable in two places on its roof, something that defied all logic—if logic was even relevant any more.

In the space of a minute, the children had pulled, from its hiding place on the woodland floor to its current position gently swinging in front of them, the very last thing Rixon expected.

'It's a caravan!' he cried. 'An actual caravan!'

'Have you never seen one before?' Faith asked him.

Of course he'd seen caravans before, being towed on the roads, where they're supposed to be.

'The cable runs all the way above us to a reinforced branch of the tree which acts as a fulcrum, Rixon. It carries the vehicle quite easily,' Russell told him.

The caravan was yellow but it was covered in so much moss, dirt and bits of branch it still looked camouflaged as it swung gently in front of Rixon's stupefied eyes.

'It's far safer for us to sleep in the sky, you see, Rixon,' Faith said earnestly. 'If there's an invasion at night, we have time to react. It's called strategy.'

'And some seagulls like kittiwakes make nests high up, so why shouldn't we?' Rose added.

At the back of his fatigued mind, Rixon wondered if he was dreaming already.

It required a big stride to cross over into the caravan. Faith used one of her long arms to reach out and open the door, and she moved across the divide like a ballet dancer. Rixon was next in line, urged forward by Rose. The surge of adrenaline that had filled Rixon's veins for the cliff-top battle had gone. But it had left something behind: bravery. Rixon had faced and conquered so many challenges that day, it was easier to face another. Without looking down, he took a step into the void and landed in the caravan. Faith's hand grabbed his elbow just as Rixon's left foot touched the floor.

'Well done,' she said.

The caravan's interior was, in fairness, far more encouraging than its exterior. There were thick rugs and soft cushions spread around everywhere. Russell and Rose made their arrivals and started to arrange beds for themselves.

'Faith, do you remember when the caravan arrived?' Rose asked.

'Oh yes, of course I do! It was so exciting. Silvester came back after dark, with a—what was it, Russell?'

'A barge,' he replied.

'Yes, he was towing it behind his own boat. And

on top of the barge was a caravan. We thought it was amazing,' Faith recalled.

'It *was* amazing . . .' Rose said wistfully.

'Silvester is the most brilliant sailor in the world. He loves his boat so much, he sleeps in it, Rixon. He told me he could never fall asleep unless he could feel the ocean beneath him,' Faith said.

'But none of us wanted to sleep in a boat, not after what happened before, you know . . .' Rose said.

Rixon nodded; he thought he understood. The last time they'd fallen asleep in a boat they'd awoken to the most horrendous situation imaginable; the night they'd lost their parents. The night they thought they'd lost everything. Only to be rescued by Silvester.

Great-uncle Silvester was a truly astonishing man, Rixon was in no doubt about that. But he was still missing something vital. What could be so threatening to the children that Silvester went to the extraordinary trouble of building a huge metal nest for them to sleep in?

Rixon, crucially, had still learned nothing more about the 'special box'.

He waited until Rose and Faith were occupied,

watching the last of the sunset from the caravan window, before he approached Russell.

'Russell, the box—I've got to know what it is,' Rixon hissed into his ear before adding for good measure, 'and remember this is my island. I've got a right to know.'

It seemed to work. Russell gave one cautious look towards the girls and then whispered back, 'Tomorrow, Rixon. Tomorrow.'

At that point, the thick quilt in the corner of the caravan which Rose had insisted Rixon should take seemed overwhelmingly inviting.

As he lay in the darkness, Rixon could soon hear the sound of deep breathing which told him the others were sleeping. At home, the last thing he'd do before he turned out the light was check the weather forecast for the following day. Now, instinctively, he felt for his laptop which would be stored under his bed. Of course it wasn't there. It was in his rucksack. But his rucksack was . . . where? Where?

In a sudden fit of panic, Rixon realized he'd left it, somewhere, on the island. With a surge of regret he realized there was nothing he could about it now.

Rixon heard the sound of the tree creaking and

branches brushing on metal, which reminded him he was stuck in a caravan in mid-air. It was amazing, it was terrifying; but there was something more powerful than the worries that were making his head pound—sheer exhaustion. Before he knew it, Rixon Webster had fallen asleep.

Chapter 9

It was Russell's hand that woke Rixon, gently shaking his shoulder. It was Russell who encouraged Rixon out of the caravan, silently urging him to step carefully. And it was Russell who led Rixon down the tree and back to one of the places he'd visited the day before.

Within minutes, they were in the museum. But Russell did not reveal another obscure historical exhibit. What he showed Rixon was very modern and extremely familiar.

'I found it in your bag,' Russell said, his voice anxious and timid. 'I won't damage it, Rixon. I mean, I didn't do anything to it . . . I know what it is . . . And you should probably choose a better password—"1,2,3,4" is quite easy to guess . . . I'm sorry.'

When he held the laptop towards Rixon,

Russell's arm trembled.

But Rixon was simply too relieved to be cross. 'Russell, thank you,' was all he said.

'I was just looking after it. I mean, it's beautiful,' Russell continued, 'but you probably shouldn't tell Faith. You see, Silvester didn't like it, and she won't go against anything Silvester said.'

'What do you mean, Russell? What didn't Silvester like?'

'Computers, technology, the Internet, the World Wide Web. He was suspicious of all of it. I wasn't, though. I passed an exam in computer science the week before we arrived here.'

'Russell, you must have been about six years old—that's impossible!'

Russell just shrugged and pulled his cap lower over his forehead. 'I didn't go out much, not for years, too sensitive to the light, they said. That's why . . .' Russell gestured towards his glasses and hat.

'Oh, right,' Rixon replied.

Russell was intriguing but Rixon had other things to focus on; he had his laptop back now. It was just possible—he dared to hope—that he could get Internet access somewhere on the island. Maybe there would be a 4G signal if he climbed up a tree? Perhaps Russell would know?

Russell, however, suddenly seemed more nervous than ever.

'I saw it Rixon, on your computer I mean. I just couldn't help it. The file was just there to click and, well, it was amazing to see it. I mean, it makes sense now. After all this time!'

Russell was so agitated he was literally bouncing up and down on the balls of his bare feet. It made no sense to Rixon.

'Russell, what are you talking about?'

'Cell Inverter 7, Rixon, Cell Inverter 7!'

With these words, Russell disappeared underneath the table in the centre of the shed, below the sagging edges of the raft. When he emerged, Russell was holding something in both hands with such care and reverence that Rixon immediately guessed what it might be.

'The special box?' he said.

Russell nodded. 'That's what we called it at home. But I know its real name is Cell Inverter 7.'

It sounded impressive. But to Rixon, it just looked like a large shoebox made of metal. At either end were ports and sockets to which wires and cables were clearly meant to be attached. On top were three tiny lightbulbs and a small hatch on hinges ready to be opened.

'I knew it was in that suitcase,' Russell continued, 'the one I grabbed in the storm, after the shipwreck. That's why I took it. I never told the others, but that's why I brought it with me ...'

As Russell's voice trailed away, Rixon wished he could see his eyes. Behind the shades, he suspected there would intense emotion, even tears. Rixon wondered if that was really why Russell always wore his sunglasses—to hide his feelings?

'But what does the box do? I mean, what is it for?' Rixon asked.

'Power,' Russell replied simply. 'It's a battery.'

It didn't look like one. The batteries Rixon used were small cylinders, generally wedged inside remote controls. This was just a box. But to Russell it was so exciting, his hands now shook again as he held it.

'I know now—the file ... I mean, I don't know how you got it on the laptop. But it explains everything. It explains how it works! The answer has been here all the time, on the island!'

'What—?' Rixon began to ask. So many questions were darting through his mind as a voice suddenly boomed across the island.

'Splinter-ball!' it cried. It was Faith, calling them.

'Oh no, quick,' Russell said, already turning to hide the 'special box'.

'Russell, wait, stop, I need to—'

'No time, no time,' Russell insisted. 'It's morning exercise.'

'Exercise . . . ?'

'Compulsory, we must go. Give me that.'

Rixon absolutely did not want to hand back his laptop. But at the same time, he had no idea where else to put it. If Faith, as Russell had told him, was really opposed to technology, there was a chance she'd confiscate it. Then there was the appalling prospect that she'd give it to Thorn for immediate destruction. That was too gruesome to contemplate. So with a heavy heart, Rixon let Russell place the computer carefully underneath the table in the middle of the museum. It was hidden alongside Cell Inverter 7.

Then they closed the shed door and ran, with Russell ordering Rixon to hurry to the beach.

The scene was being set for 'Splinterball'.

Faith was finishing the markings—a large circular pitch drawn in the sand with a branch. Inside, four upright sticks stood a metre apart to make a square. Four tennis balls also lay on the sand. Rixon had no idea what the rules might be. But he knew one thing: Thorn was back.

'Russell, we haven't had our cups of tea. When are you going to make the fire?' Thorn's morning rage seemed to be aimed at Russell—that was something, at least. He ignored Rixon, except for one brief glare.

'It doesn't matter. We'll have breakfast afterwards,' Faith declared. 'I'm in the mood for beans on toast. Rose, is there any bread?'

Rose shook her head. 'Faith, you know there isn't,' she replied.

'Well, never mind,' Faith said, clapping her hands. 'OK, let's have teams. Rixon, you can go with Rose.'

Rixon immediately felt relieved—Rose was friendly. But then he realized what this implied: if he was on Rose's team, then he would be playing against Thorn. If Splinterball bore any similarity to American football, or rugby, he was doomed.

Rixon was desperately wondering if he could suggest something else; if there was some way he could clear the beach and divert the children's attention away from their game. But in the end, he didn't need to. The hurricane did it for him.

The sea was the first clue. It looked as though it was bubbling. Little white peaks were forming and foaming on the surface.

Then it was the trees, groaning. At first it sounded like a librarian urgently insisting on quiet, but the 'shush' grew in volume until it was almost a yell in Rixon's ear. He turned towards the centre of the island. The trees were swaying, but they were twisting too, as if they didn't know which way to bend in the wind.

A swarm of leaves now flew towards Rixon, brushing his face, his shirt billowing out behind him, collecting the wind like a sail. But then the gale changed direction. Now it was coming down right on top of him, as if someone was holding an enormous hairdryer directly above his head.

By the time Rixon looked around for the others, they'd almost made it back to the clearing. Faith was gesturing to him frantically. He could hear her words, just.

'Quick, to the store! We must . . . underground . . . safe!'

Rixon understood where they were going. But he wasn't going with them.

He'd just seen something in the sky.

The sound had intensified. There was a higher-pitched noise. A whirring sound, like something spinning at incredible speed.

Rixon was concentrating so hard, he was only aware of Rose at his side when she grabbed his arm.

'Oww!'

'Rixon, sorry—I mean, come on! You can't stand here. It's too dangerous! We must go underground when a big storm comes. It's safer there. Come on!' She tugged his shirt with all her strength, but Rixon stood firm.

'No, no, Rose. It's not a storm. Look!'

Rixon pointed to the sky and, despite her fears, Rose did look. Rixon felt his arm being gripped once again, and squeezed so tightly it hurt.

'Rixon, what . . . what is that?' Rose had to shout now, the noise was so loud.

Rixon lowered his head so his mouth was almost touching Rose's ear. He only said one word and spoke slowly and deliberately, to make sure she understood.

'Helicopter!'

And then Rixon grabbed the back of Rose's T-shirt and ran, pulling her with him, closing his eyes against the grains of sand which flew up and stung their faces.

They didn't stop until they reached the trunk of the first tree they could throw themselves behind. It was safe there, Rixon thought, to hide and watch. As he looked up into the sky, Rixon had to acknowledge one indisputable fact: someone else had found the island that didn't exist.

Chapter 10

Rixon had actually only seen helicopters on television. But at least he had some idea of what was happening, unlike Rose.

'Look, look! It's falling, it's falling! Rixon, it's falling!'

'It's landing, Rose, it's coming down to land!' he yelled back at her. 'It's what they do.'

The wall, although concealing Splinter Island from those approaching by sea, did not hamper arrivals from above. There was no roof to it. But clearly, from Rose's reaction, nobody had ever come in this way before.

The noise of the helicopter's descent was so loud that the silence which followed felt shocking. Rixon's eyes were fixed on the helicopter which now stood directly in the middle of the circle, drawn for Splinterball. It was as if Faith had unwittingly sketched out a helipad. Rose, however, was still searching in the sky.

'It's scared all the gulls,' she said anxiously. 'They don't mind aeroplanes; they're much quieter. If the gulls hear one, they come and cover the top of the island like a cloud, to protect us.'

Rixon turned to her, 'Are you serious, Rose?'

'Yes, of course. It's like another curtain that they make above the island. There are only a few planes, now and then. But, that . . .'

Rose's eyes turned nervously back towards the helicopter; so did Rixon's. When the door of the cockpit opened, Rose gasped and grabbed Rixon's arm.

But Rixon barely noticed the fingernails gripping his skin. Every bit of his attention was focused on the man who was now getting out of the helicopter. He was bending down to avoid the blades. He was smoothing his short, grey hair. He was beginning to look at his new surroundings.

'Rixon, come on! We must hide!' Rose screamed in his ear.

But Rixon didn't move; he didn't even turn his head. He was trying to understand what he saw, because it seemed impossible. He was looking at someone he'd known his entire life.

'Rose,' Rixon said, 'that's my dad.'

When Rose ran, Rixon didn't try to stop her. He had a fleeting worry about spears being gathered but really there was only room for one thought in Rixon's mind.

His dad was here.

There was a time when Rixon would build his whole week around the Sundays he'd spend with his father. He'd plan the day in advance, imagine their activities, and then, once the day was done, review every moment in the week that followed. Each ice cream would be retasted, each movie rewatched, each ruined castle invaded again in those mock battles his dad directed and Rixon replayed in his mind.

But he'd been small then. His dad had cared then, he'd still lived nearby.

When the weeks of his dad's absence started to become months, Rixon worried terribly. His mum always offered the same explanation: 'It's not you, Rixon; your dad loves you. It's just his job.'

It became very clear to Rixon that if his dad did indeed love him, then he loved his job more.

It would have been easier to understand if Rixon actually knew what his father did for a living, but it was all shrouded in secrecy. Even his mum said she didn't know completely; David Webster was 'employed by the government' and he was 'keeping our country safe'. That's how Rixon's mum explained it. To Rixon, this all seemed thrilling and he would have been excited to discuss it with his dad in his kitchen, or his back garden or even walking down to the park.

But David Webster was never at those places.

He was, however, on Splinter Island. And to Rixon that still seemed impossible. Even though he could now hear his dad calling his name.

'Rixon! Rixon, you're here! I can't believe it; thank God!'

Rixon had moved from the tree trunk so that he was in full view. Now that his dad could see him, Rixon really didn't know what to do. Somewhere in his mind he thought he should be sprinting towards his dad and throwing his arms around him. But it had been forever since he'd last done that. And something about the whole situation left Rixon feeling deeply uneasy. How had his father found him? How, for that matter, had he acquired a helicopter?

In the end, it was David Webster who marched forward. His clipped grey hair hardly moved in the sea-breeze but his arms swung by his side. Like a soldier, Rixon thought. His dad was wearing a black jacket with a zip in the middle and he carried, Rixon noticed, an enormous phone in his left hand.

This made their meeting even more awkward.

'Oh, sorry,' David Webster said, as he attempted to put his arm around Rixon's shoulders and ended up poking the aerial in Rixon's right ear. 'It's a satphone,' he explained. 'Get you reception anywhere, this thing.'

'Oh, right,' Rixon replied. There was so much to say he didn't know how to begin. 'Dad, why are you here?' he eventually asked.

'Me?' his dad retorted. 'Rixon, I should be asking you the very same question!'

So Rixon explained, or at least he gave a version of the extraordinary events of the previous twenty-four hours. He stressed that he'd 'borrowed' a boat to get here. His dad raised his eyebrows at that, and in a few other places, but he let Rixon finish.

'Well, your mother has been worried sick,' David Webster said. 'All she had was that half-baked phone conversation which she barely heard—you telling her you'd found Splinter

Island. There's no record of it anywhere on the Internet . . . Did you know that?'

Rixon nodded.

'There's been a coastguard boat out, only they didn't know where to search, did they? They can't see through walls, even pretend ones. Luckily, I'm connected. You see, Rixon, I can get things.' He motioned towards the helicopter on the beach behind him. 'I got Billy too, best pilot in the business. I don't know anyone else who would have spotted this place. He's a genius, Billy. He's discreet too.'

Rixon could see there was man sitting inside the cockpit. He had long white hair tied in a ponytail and he was reading a magazine.

His dad, meanwhile, was edging towards the sea, looking up to the sky and then down at the phone in his hand. 'Just trying to find the best spot . . . need a clean line of sight, away from the trees,' he said. 'Ah, got it.'

David Webster stopped right on the shoreline. He punched a few keys on his satphone, held it to his ear, and said, 'I've got him. No, he's fine. No, call off the search, no need. The police have got better things to do. Look, will you phone his mother? No, I haven't got time. Yes, we'll be airborne soon. Five minutes. Bye.'

David Webster clipped the phone to his belt, put his hands on his hips, and turned his head to survey the island around him.

'We circled the coast for almost two hours before we found you, Rixon. I can't believe this place exists . . . Those huge curtains? Incredible. And Silvester put them up, to protect the seagulls? Is that what you said, Rixon?'

Rixon nodded, trying to remember exactly what he'd told his father and what he'd left out.

'Silvester was a weird character, mad I reckon,' David Webster continued. 'I only met him once, at our wedding. Your mother insisted on inviting him. He turned up on a horse. Literally, a horse!' David Webster snorted at the memory. 'Mind you, I never dreamt he was capable of hiding a whole island!'

Rixon looked at his father and wondered if he really knew him. His dad had discovered that Rixon was missing, summoned a helicopter (plus pilot), used it for himself (for hours) to find Splinter Island, and then instructed the emergency services to call off their search. It seemed as though David Webster had the world at his fingertips . . . using the keys of his satphone.

'Can I call Mum?' Rixon asked.

'No point,' his dad answered, his eyes locked on the sky. 'We'll have you home soon. You know it was such a stupid thing to do, Rixon. I mean, how long do you think you would have survived out here, all on your own?'

All on his own . . . Rixon thought about the children. He hadn't mentioned them to his dad. He still wasn't sure exactly why they were hiding but he knew there was a very good reason. There were secrets here, big secrets, and Rixon was far from sure if his dad was the person to be trusted with them.

But he also knew that the children of Splinter Island could not remain hidden forever.

'Dad, listen. About being here alone. That's the thing—' he hesitated for a moment '—I'm not.'

The baffled look in his dad's eyes was the last thing Rixon remembered.

Rixon did not see it coming either; how could he? As far as Rixon knew, all the others were hiding in the underground store. To get from there to the coastline they would have to follow the path through the island's interior, find a gap in the thick wall of vegetation and then stride across the beach, fully visible.

But there was another way. If you were strong enough, and brave enough, you could clamber down to a ledge on the cliff at the wild coast on the far side of the island. Jumping off there was only for the fearless. But from that point it was possible, if you possessed the power and determination, to swim round to the beach where Rixon and his father stood. It would take approximately fifteen minutes.

Not only had someone dared to undertake this, but he had finished the journey underwater.

Thorn burst from the sea like a dolphin leaping from the depths. He was so quick, he was so silent, that Rixon's dad barely had time to turn his head. He had absolutely no chance to get away.

Thorn hurled himself onto the man's back and wrapped his left arm around his neck, pulling him back towards the sea. David Webster tried to plant his feet in the sand, but Thorn was too strong, he just dragged him to the water. Within seconds Rixon's dad was knee deep in the sea. He crashed the water with his free arms as he tried to grab hold of Thorn, his fists sending plumes of spray into the air around them. But Rixon's dad was panicking while Thorn had a plan; there was only going to be one winner.

Rixon screamed, 'Thorn, no!'

He was about to dash forward to try to end the fight, when he saw something glinting in Thorn's hand. Still clinging to David Webster's neck with his left arm, Thorn had reached into the waistband of his shorts with his right hand and pulled out a knife.

It was small and it was sharp—an ordinary kitchen tool. But in the hands of Thorn it could, Rixon feared, do anything.

'OK, Thorn, it's OK. Nobody is going to harm you,' Rixon said reassuringly. 'This man is my dad.'

Rixon had intended these words to calm the situation. They had the opposite effect.

'Ha! Another one! It's not your island! You can't take it!'

Rixon watched with a gasp as Thorn raised the knife into the air. But he wasn't the only one who'd seen it.

'Easy now, son, you don't really want to hurt someone do you . . .?'

He'd dashed from the helicopter so quietly Rixon had no idea he'd even moved until he heard that voice right next to him.

The pilot—'Billy', his dad had called him—

was now standing just a metre away. He looked incredibly calm, Rixon thought. He was wearing a kind of all-in-one green suit. Rolled up in his back pocket was a magazine with a picture of a motorbike on the cover. Billy held his hands out of front of him with his palms open, facing the sky.

'Now come on, son, you're not going to beat the both of us.' He motioned his hand towards Rixon's dad who was making strange noises from this throat. Thorn now drew his right hand upwards so that the blade of the knife was level with the David Webster's eyes.

Billy decided he couldn't wait any longer.

He began running towards Thorn and then instantly jumped back, yelling in pain.

'Whaaat!'

Billy was looking at his left leg, and specifically at the spear that was now stuck there.

There wasn't much blood. His jumpsuit came with thick trousers. But the pain must have been incredible. So, Rixon was astonished that Billy almost seemed amused.

'Two tours of Iraq, three years running aid drops over the Congo, and I get hit for the first time in my life here! On a lump of the rock in the sea!'

He pulled out the spear and held it up to his

eye, shook his head, and smiled. 'Who threw this?' Billy shouted.

Faith stepped out from behind the very tree where Rixon and Rose had been hiding just a few minutes before. 'I did,' she said, proudly, 'we armed ourselves in the storeroom, and then came to try and find Thorn.'

'Well, that was some shot,' Billy said. 'Have you ever thought of the army?'

Faith looked puzzled for a moment. 'Which army? My aim with the left is bad so, when I've got a spear, I normally think of my right one.'

Billy threw back his head and roared with laughter.

Faith looked perplexed but then smiled too.

The whole episode seemed to have cooled some of Thorn's fury. He had lowered the knife but was still grasping David Webster's neck.

'Help, please help . . .' Rixon's dad gasped.

These words only made Thorn tighten his grip. In a panic, Rixon knew he had to do something. But when he started speaking Rixon found himself making a promise he had no idea how to keep.

'Thorn, please let go of my dad. He's going to bring you food and everything you need on the island.'

Thorn just grunted. 'Riddles,' he said. 'You're tricking me.'

'No, no,' Rixon insisted. 'My dad is a powerful man; he virtually runs a whole country. I mean, look, he can even get that!' He motioned his arms desperately towards the helicopter.

'It's true, son, think about it,' Billy said. 'He can help you, we can help you.'

Still Thorn held on. There was only one person whose instructions he would accept.

'Thorn, let him go.' Faith declared solemnly. Those words worked. Thorn reluctantly released David Webster.

'What on earth—' was all Rixon's dad managed to mumble before he was consumed by a fit of coughing. Faith was looking straight at Rixon.

'Rixon, this man is your father? He is an intruder.'

'It's OK, Faith, don't worry.'

'Rixon, who are these kids? Did you bring them with you? They're out of control . . .' David Webster was looking anxiously at Thorn but also across the beach, where they could see Rose and Russell approaching, 'Where are their parents?' he demanded.

'Is he riddling us?' Thorn replied furiously.

'Dad, they don't have parents and they didn't come with me,' Rixon said frantically, trying to defuse the situation before it all boiled over again. He paused just for a second, before deciding that all he could do was tell was the truth. 'You see, Dad, they live here. Silvester looks after them—well, he did.'

'What?' His dad's expression was complete bewilderment.

Faith, meanwhile, looked livid. 'Rixon, this man means danger,' she said, pointing to his dad, 'and unless you explain how he can help us, then I will have to tell Thorn to attack.'

Thorn was still loitering ominously, right alongside David Webster.

Rixon took a deep breath and tried to focus his mind. At that moment, everything seemed to hang in the balance. Even with Billy's help he wasn't sure that they could outfight the Splinter Islanders, not with Thorn on their side.

'Faith, you need help, you must admit that,' Rixon began. He saw Faith's shoulders visibly stiffen and her eyes narrow. 'I mean, you've done a fantastic job. Silvester would be proud of you. He would be proud of all of you,' Rixon said quickly, 'but you've got to look to the future.

I mean, you've got to eat.' Faith said nothing but her eyes turned towards the ground.

Rose came up beside Faith, and now spoke softly but firmly. 'There's not much, not much at all, in the store. You know that, Faith.'

Rixon continued, 'You can't live without food. I know Silvester was going to make the farm better, to help you grow things, but he's . . . gone.'

Thorn growled an objection but Rixon saw Rose nod slowly. He pressed on. 'My dad will help. He will get you things, all sorts of things. Won't you, Dad?'

When Rixon turned towards his dad, he hoped and prayed that his father would help. He needed support. But his dad's eyes were wild. His words told Rixon everything he needed to know; his dad was interested in one person—himself.

'I don't take orders,' David Webster said. 'I give them.'

Now he wasn't even looking at Rixon; he was just staring at each of the children in turn, darting his eyes between them frantically and then shaking his head in astonishment.

'How long?' he barked. 'How long have they been here, these children?'

Rixon could feel the agitation growing, Faith

had her spear in her hand and she was starting to raise it.

'Dad, it doesn't matter . . .'

'How long, Rixon? I must know.'

'Five years,' Rixon answered hurriedly. 'They told me they've been here five years.'

'Aha, it fits! It actually fits!' David jumped forwards when he said these words, the index finger of his right hand pointing triumphantly towards the sun.

'Dad, dad, what are you doing?' Rixon could see Thorn was still holding his knife and had raised his arm, he was now looking at Faith for instructions. But nothing would stop David Webster.

'If what I think is true,' Rixon's dad continued, 'and as crazy as it seems, I think it must be true, then I can assure these children that whatever they possibly want the government will provide for them.'

'Really?' Rixon said, watching his dad raise both of his hands skywards in a fresh display of elation.

'Oh yes, Rixon, oh yes. The whole world's going to go wild when I tell them; David Webster has just solved the biggest mystery of the century.'

Chapter 11

Splinter Island was still gripped by a mood of suspicion and thinly-veiled hostility. The person who helped improve the atmosphere was Billy. He'd briefly returned to the helicopter to fetch what he described as 'emergency rations'.

The arrival of cereal bars, apples, and a tube of mints had distracted the children. When Billy produced a small bottle of lemonade from the depths of his trouser pocket, it was further encouragement. Faith agreed to Rixon's suggestion that there should be a meeting where hopefully his dad would explain things.

Rixon, more than anyone, was desperate for explanations.

His dad had spent the past twenty minutes on his phone conducting urgent, whispered conversations. He was 'cross-checking and fact-blasting,' he'd explained. Rixon was still confused. But he was also determined. This was, he reminded himself, *his* island.

So it turned out like this: Rixon's dad sat on a rock in the middle of the clearing, Billy the pilot stood just behind him, Rixon himself sat just to the side, and the children of Splinter Island lined themselves up a few metres away. They stood together, as a team, in opposition. Each of them held a spear.

'Dad, do you know who these children are?' Rixon began. The idea seemed absurd, but it was what his father had suggested.

'Yes, I do,' David Webster said, the manic intensity now returning to his eyes, 'but firstly I need to confirm one thing. The parents, where are they?'

It was clear than none of the children was going to answer, so Rixon did, hoping that his dad would react sensitively.

'They all died, Dad . . .' Rixon said softly.

David Webster did not react sensitively. 'So, they cheated justice did they? Well, traitors used to be put to death, I suppose.'

'Dad!' Rixon exclaimed. 'You can't say that!'

His dad waved away Rixon's protests with

one sweep of his arm and turned to stare at the children in front of him. 'You're the science kids, aren't you? Your parents, they're the ones who tried to escape, didn't they? They stole the secrets and then disappeared!'

The children had been simmering; now they boiled over.

'Lies! You're lying!'

'They didn't steal anything, it was their invention!'

'Get off our island! You don't know anything!'

Rixon thought there would be a fight within seconds. Fortunately, Billy had exactly the same idea and placed himself between David Webster and the children, his arms outstretched.

'Now, now, there's no need for fireworks. David here is going to be nice, isn't he?' Billy ended this sentence with a glare in the direction of Rixon's dad.

David Webster said nothing but he was running his fingers around his neck and remembering— Rixon thought—what Thorn could do. 'All right, I didn't mean to offend anyone . . .' he eventually mumbled.

'I know Russell's mum and dad were brilliant scientists and inventors,' Rixon said hurriedly, trying to say something positive.

'They all were,' Russell answered. 'My mum and dad, Faith's mum, Rose and Thorn's parents—all of them. They came from different countries, but they all worked together. They spoke English together and they spent their lives together.'

'These names,' David Webster interrupted, 'who gave them to you? If you could tell me, please?' he added grudgingly.

'Silvester named them,' Rixon explained, 'when he rescued them. He found them, when their boat . . . crashed.'

'Boat crashed, yes, of course . . .' David Webster nodded to himself. 'That's how they left the country—right, it all makes sense. But, if you'll allow me, I'm just going to say a few different names. Let's see if they ring any bells, yes?'

Rixon looked at the children. They didn't say a word but their faces were impenetrable, like steel.

'Now, twins; well, you don't look much alike but if you're the same age, you must be Martha and Peter O'Connell. Sophia Bergen, tall like your mum. I met her once, you know. Yes, that's you. And then Ernesto Alvarez—it must be. The descriptions at the time said you always wore sunglasses.'

The children exchanged alarmed looks, they edged close together but they did not utter a word to dispute what David Webster had just said.

But Rixon had to have an explanation.

'Dad, Dad, what are you talking about?'

'I was part of the investigation, Rixon, trying to repair the damage done by those fools in the police. If the National Secure Borders Force had been in charge, we'd have been fine. That's my department. But the police officers who were on guard duty let them slip away—unbelievable! The great science scandal, the papers called it. Journalists had a field day.'

Of course, the newspapers had called it that; Rixon had seen the headlines! This was the story in the clippings in the brown envelope, the one Arnold Crump had given him just as he'd left the lawyer's office! The story David Webster was now feverishly retelling.

'Just when they were perfecting the battery— the one that would save the world—those scientists disappeared. And they took their kids with them too. None of them ever to be seen again—' David Webster folded his arms and slowly shook his head in wonder '—until now . . .'

The children did not rush towards David Webster in a fit of anger. They simply huddled even closer together. To Rixon's surprise, he saw Faith place her spear on the ground and reach out to pull the others near her. When she spoke, her voice was forceful but calm.

'I know why they went, I was old enough to understand. Everyone wanted the invention. They wanted it for weapons, for war, for money. It wasn't supposed to be for that. It was made to save the world.'

David Webster chuckled bitterly. 'Well, they could sell it to the highest bidder, that's for sure. Perhaps that's why they ran off with it? Who paid for the labs and all the research that made the super battery? Our government, that's who.'

'Hang on a minute,' Rixon said, wanting to avoid another confrontation but desperate to understand it all. 'Was it really that important, a battery?'

'Of course it was, Rixon—think!' his dad exclaimed. 'The world is running out of resources. We need aeroplanes to cross continents. We need tanks to protect our borders. We need lorries to deliver all the things we eat, wear, and use. We need electric cars to take us wherever we want to go. Imagine if they all used a battery which never ran out? That was the invention!'

'I watched my dad trying to make it work every day of his life.'

It took David Webster a few seconds to realize that the deepest voice on Splinter island belonged to its smallest citizen.

'You know? You, Ernesto—I mean, Russell— you know how it works?' David Webster's eyes glared with a new mania.

Russell just shrugged and pushed the sunglasses back on the bridge of his nose. Rixon realized something: at that moment, only two people in the world knew that Cell Inverter 7 actually existed; only two people knew that it was actually just metres away from where they were standing! Russell knew, Rixon knew. Rixon's dad didn't.

But David Webster had the scent. He had heard something in Russell's voice or seen something in his body language that told him to keep up the chase. He took another step towards Russell.

'I should remind you that if there is any information you are withholding, it will have very serious consequences,' he said. 'I am quite prepared to use the full force of the law against you . . . against all of you.'

That was enough for Thorn. He lifted up his spear with both hands and held it across his chest. He then hurled it forward so it struck David Webster in the ribs. As Rixon's dad staggered backwards, Faith also picked up her spear. Billy danced in between them, while Rixon tried to grab Thorn's shoulder and missed.

'Stop!' Russell boomed. The shock of his voice, delivered at such volume, made everyone freeze.

'You are wrong, Mr Webster,' Russell said calmly and with conviction. 'What you said is wrong. Splinter island is over twelve nautical miles from the mainland, so your laws have no influence here; you cannot enforce them.'

'What?' Rixon's dad replied, pausing for a second and trying to force a laugh. 'Are you joking?'

'No, I don't think he is,' Billy said. He gestured towards Russell, and a smile of admiration, Rixon thought, was just playing across his lips. 'To be fair, I think the lad's right. I actually had the same thought myself as we flew over.'

A fierce objection was forming on David Webster's lips, but at that moment, another noise filled the air. It was a sound which would have seemed so familiar back at home Rixon would probably have ignored it. But on Splinter Island it was like the sound of an alien invasion.

David Webster's phone was ringing.

'Yes?' he answered abruptly, clutching the phone to his ear in irritation. But as soon as the conversation began, his tone changed dramatically. 'Oh, now? Right, but you see . . . Yes, we do have him, but there's something else, something very important . . . what? Can't anyone else? No, no, but—'

Whoever was speaking on the other end had hung up. David Webster punched the screen of his phone in rage. 'Of all the curses,' he seethed.

'Who was it?' Billy asked.

'The palace,' David Webster replied through gritted teeth. 'They say "you know who" needs the helicopter, right away, immediately!'

'Ah . . .' Billy said with a nod, 'their highnesses and the high life. Well, you know what that means?'

David Webster did. He sighed deeply and kicked the ground so viciously that, for a few seconds, he was surrounded by a cloud of sand.

'Right, come on, Rixon,' his dad said abruptly. 'We'll get you home and then I'll think of what we do with this lot.' He motioned towards the children. 'Two dozen police should do it, and dogs, in case Muscles over there gets any ideas.'

Thorn glared back at him.

Rixon looked at the children, and then he turned back towards his father.

'Rixon, come on—now,' David Webster demanded.

Rixon looked down at the sand. He was standing on his beach, on his island. If he left now, would he ever come back? The man who was talking to him seemed less of a father than ever. In fact, he seemed like a bully, shouting orders. And Rixon was not in the mood to be bullied.

He knew what his dad wanted; he wanted Cell Inverter 7 and he wanted glory. David Webster certainly didn't care about the children of Splinter Island. Rixon was increasingly certain that he didn't he really care about his own son.

The two little words which left Rixon's mouth felt like the biggest he'd ever spoken.

'No, Dad,' Rixon said.

'What? What did you say?' his dad yelled back at him. 'You can't stay here, Rixon. Are you mad?'

'No, Dad,' Rixon repeated. 'I'm not mad.'

'And he's not going.' Faith had moved alongside Rixon and she had her spear in its horizontal ready position, tilted back, its tip level with her shoulder.

'Easy, now,' Billy murmured. 'I know what you can do with that.'

'Stand aside,' David Webster instructed. 'Let Rixon leave.'

'He's not going,' Faith repeated.

'Faith, are you sure? I mean—' Thorn began to object.

'Be quiet, Thorn, we need him here.'

'He's coming with me; he's coming home,' David Webster insisted.

'If we let Rixon go with you now, then how do we know you'll ever come back?' Faith explained. 'And you're supposed to be bringing us all that food, remember?'

Now Thorn nodded his head, understanding the plan. He too lifted his spear and pointed it at David Webster. Rixon realized he was a bargaining tool. He felt as though he was being taken hostage on his own island.

But he was powerless and so, for that matter, was his father.

David Webster made his right hand into a fist

but the only thing he punched was the palm of his left.

'Come on, Billy, if we're late, there will be hell to pay. When you've finished with the royal games, we'll come back here and finish this one!' He turned on his heel and marched towards the helicopter.

Billy began to follow him but then paused for a second, turning back towards the children. 'What's your favourite kind of chocolate?' he asked Rose.

'Kind? You mean there are different kinds?' she replied, in genuine astonishment.

Billy laughed and jogged to the cockpit. Thirty seconds later, the blades were rotating. Within a minute, the helicopter was just a dot in the sky. As he watched it disappear, Rixon felt proud that he'd stood up to his father, but the energy he'd summoned up for that confrontation was starting to drain away.

At that moment, what he also felt was Rose's hand on his shoulder. 'Are you OK, Rixon?' she asked gently.

Rixon turned and smiled. 'I'm OK, I think,' he said. 'I just don't know what to do now ...'

'No, there's no one to tell us, is there?' Rose

replied.

She was thinking of Silvester, Rixon knew, and so—it became clear—was someone else.

'We need to go to the museum!' Russell was standing in a most unusual pose, hands on hips, cap tilted to the sky. Rixon had never seen him like that before.

'Russell, we most certainly do not need to go there; what I think is this—' Faith began.

But Russell interrupted her. He raised his hand and his voice, and his next words were so sudden and unexpected that they stopped everything.

'We need to hear what Silvester has to say,' Russell told them. He started walking, and, in stunned silence, they all followed.

Chapter 12

Rixon remembered that the others, even Faith, considered the museum to be Russell's territory. Once they reached the rickety old shed, precariously propped up by the metal wind turbine, Russell quickly took charge.

'Silvester left the most precious things in my care,' Russell began, 'to be stored here.'

'Yes, the raft, we know,' Faith answered.

'No, not just that. He also gave me this.'

He'd actually hidden it in the raft, tucked inside its plastic folds as it sagged on the table. Now Russell proudly held it aloft as if it was a piece of rock he'd brought from the moon.

'Rixon, you know what this is?'

He did. It was completely ordinary. His mum still had dozens of them.

'Sure, it's a DVD,' Rixon said, nodding towards

the silver disc in Russell's hand. 'But what's on it?'

'I don't know, not exactly,' Russell admitted. 'I mean, there was no way of knowing, not until now, not until we had this . . .'

He turned, crouched, and reached under the table for the device Rixon knew was there. But when Russell produced the laptop, the others were stunned.

'Russell, where did you get that from?' Rose gasped.

'It's forbidden, you shouldn't have it,' Faith fumed.

'Yes, yes, but it's not mine, it's Rixon's,' Russell explained. 'He brought it with him and, besides, you will want to see this, Faith. I don't care what you say, you will want to see this. It will play on your computer, won't it, Rixon?'

He wasn't sure at first; Rixon had never tried to use such old technology. But there was a slot on the side which sprang open, and the DVD fitted snugly.

'Russell, we should not be doing this. Silvester said technology was dangerous—' Faith insisted.

'No, Faith,' Russell interrupted, 'don't you see? This is Silvester.'

'What?' Faith cried.

'But—?' Rose blustered.

'Riddles . . .' Thorn hissed.

'On this DVD, it's him, it's Silvester!' Russell went on excitedly. 'It's the message he left us, the message he told me we should play if he ever . . . went.'

Silence followed, and Rixon could see from the children's faces that they were flabbergasted. They were also desperate to see if Russell was right.

When Rixon pressed Play, the reaction was instantaneous.

'Silvester!' Rose gasped.

'He's there!' Faith cried.

'How?!' Thorn exclaimed.

They were watching the face they knew and loved. For Rixon, it was the first time he'd actually seen the man who'd changed the whole course of his life.

He was old, his hair was long and white, and his beard grew like icicles, pointing down his chin. But Silvester's blue eyes were bright. At that precise moment, they sparkled with confusion.

'Are you working? Are you on? They told me it was simple, in the shop: best DVD camcorder ever made, they said,' Silvester muttered. 'Wretched thing. I told them I only needed you for five minutes . . .'

'Who is he speaking to?' Rose whispered.

'The camcorder,' Rixon answered, as the picture wobbled. 'He's not sure how to work it.'

Silvester finally seemed satisfied. He leaned back, settled himself in his chair, and cleared his throat.

'Splinter Islanders, live free!' Silvester suddenly boomed, slowly raising his right hand to his forehead in a stately salute.

To Rixon's amazement, all four of the children then stood tall and answered in unison, 'We live free!', returning the salute as they did so.

Rixon briefly wondered if they knew this was a recording. Could they possibly imagine Silvester was really there, right in front of them?

If they did, Silvester put them right with his next sentence.

'I am filming this now because at some point in the future, I will leave you . . . If you are watching this, then I am gone, dead. Actually, I don't know how you will watch this . . .' Silvester paused for a second, looked away from the camera, and stroked his white beard. 'I suppose

I never thought things through, not properly. I always act first, think later; that's my problem.' He smiled to himself. 'But I know Russell will find a way, somehow, to make this work. I always thought we'd find a way. Perhaps I was wrong . . .' He paused again. 'Yes, I need to apologize.'

Rixon heard a murmur among the children.

'I could have taken you back, I should have done,' Silvester continued, 'I went to the mainland many times to make arrangements. But every time, as soon as I reached shore, there would be news: another war, another bomb, another government making another rule about what children should learn!' Silvester threw up his arms in exasperation. 'Did I want you to go back to that? No, not with the danger I knew you'd be in. You see, I knew who you were, I knew why you were coming here. Faith, your mother— she'd already contacted me a year before. I never told you that, did I . . . ?'

Rixon turned to look at Faith, her eyes narrowed in deep concentration as she watched Silvester talking. 'She knew about the mines, you see; she knew about the cobalt. She'd found out about Splinter Island. There are still records buried in museums, old mining maps, if you look hard enough. The mines made people scared hundreds of years ago. When men came to work here and never returned home, people thought this place was evil. Ha! Well your mother didn't, Faith. She reckoned it was perfect. Splinter Island was the place, the only place, she and the other scientists could get the cobalt to make the super battery work. And, think about it—who in the world was going to find them on an island that didn't exist?'

'Cobalt,' Rose whispered. 'He means the special blue crystal?'

'Yes,' Russell replied.

Now Silvester's voice slowed and his eyes lowered towards the floor. 'I'm so very sorry I couldn't save them, your parents. I had a choice, you see. A terrible choice. In that storm, in that wretched, wild blackness, I could either go after the wreckage from the boat or rescue the raft, the one they'd put you in, the lifeboat . . .' Silvester slowly lifted his head back to the camera. 'I chose you,' he said.

Russell's expression gave nothing away, as ever. But in the eyes of the others, even Thorn, Rixon could clearly see tears.

Silvester continued to speak. Some of the

things he'd told the children before, but he wanted to set the record straight. He wanted to explain everything. Silvester thought their parents' boat had been sabotaged, bombed. He knew the scientists had a fantastic new invention, and he feared that if the children returned home, they'd be kidnapped by someone desperate for information. The battery was so important, there were people who'd do anything to get it, or destroy it. If one company or country had the battery it could produce endless clean energy; it could control the world. But the super battery would also ruin people. Anybody making money from traditional energy would be out of business overnight. All those companies making millions of petrol and diesel cars, for example— nobody would want them.

'I knew the battery was incredibly brilliant but devastatingly dangerous,' Silvester said, 'when I saw that Russell had brought it ashore, in that suitcase you clung onto, Russell. I panicked. I considered throwing the battery into the ocean!' Silvester paused, lost in thought, and stroked his beard again, his fingers moving slowly and deliberately. 'Perhaps I should have destroyed it. But I know how vitally important it could be in the right hands. There was a memory stick thing in the suitcase too. I took it to the mainland, plugged it in a computer, you know, imported it or whatever you say. Well, it was all nonsense to me. I couldn't read it, couldn't understand it but I thought it might be important. So, I left it with the only trustworthy person I can think of: Arnold.'

'Arnold Crump! The lawyer, he gave it to me!'

'Shush, Rixon, we need to hear!' Russell hissed at him.

'As for the battery itself, well, I didn't dare bring that to the mainland. I entrusted it to the person who rescued it, the person who would not let go of the suitcase even as I dragged him off that raft. Russell, thank you for being the guardian of Cell Inverter 7.'

'What? Does that mean—?' Rose exclaimed.

'You've got it? You've had it, all this time?' Faith interrupted, her question sounding more like an accusation.

Russell just nodded. 'That's why it was my place, here, the museum,' he said. 'That's why Silvester made it that way . . .'

Faith wanted to say more but her attention was drawn back to the computer screen; Silvester was speaking again.

'Now, Splinter Islanders, I must warn you, I must prepare you. There will be somebody coming to see you. I don't know how he will reach you; I don't know even if he will . . . I hope he does. You see, it's the biggest lesson I've learned in my life; you can't trust adults. Grown-ups ruin the world.' He smiled ruefully for a second. 'I couldn't leave my island to you in my will, Splinter Islanders, because you're dead. That's what the world thinks. And that's how you must remain. You're safest that way, do you see? If I named you in my will then it would reveal everything—the world would know you were still alive.'

Rixon understood. And he also knew what was coming next.

'So, I left my island to the only other child I knew,' Silvester said. Then the old man threw his arms up again, as if he was amazed by his own words. 'I didn't know what else to do. I have become so cut off from the world now, the only thing I can trust is the future. And he is family too. Family is very important, I've told you that every day that I've known you. So please welcome him, if he comes. His name is Rixon Webster.'

They all turned to look at Rixon now, as if they

were seeing him for the first time. There was a look in Faith's eyes that Rixon couldn't quite read, but it made him nervous.

'The last thing, and the most important thing,' Silvester continued, his voice now rising, 'is that you must stick together. If I'd taken you back to the mainland, you would have been split apart, taken into care, to foster homes, separated. I couldn't have that, no. Not after what you'd been through. I know you would have hated it. I know you belong together . . .'

Silvester sighed and sat back in his chair. He looked exhausted. Rixon was trying to guess his age. At times, during the video, he'd been bursting with life and energy. Now his eyes looked as though they'd witnessed a hundred years, encased in the white frame of hair and beard. Silvester bent forward and reached out to turn off the camcorder. At the last moment, he stopped. He drew his back up straight, tilted his fingers into a salute, and gave his people their greeting once more.

'Splinter Islanders, live free,' Silvester said. But his voice was no longer a passionate call to arms. He sounded as if he was trying to convince them, or convince himself.

'We live free,' the children replied softly, in unison.

Then Silvester was gone. The screen of Rixon's laptop was black. Each of the children, Rixon sensed, was holding onto his image in their minds. None of them wanted to speak because it would shatter the illusion that Silvester was still there, among them. But for Rixon there was one question he needed to be answered, and he knew who to ask.

'Russell, can you make it work?'

Russell just nodded. Without speaking, he reached under the table and retrieved the special box, Cell Inverter 7, the super battery. All its names amounted to the same thing; it was the invention to change the world. And yet nobody had ever even seen it being used.

'I'll show you,' Russell said.

Faith fumed with indignation.

'How could you, Russell? How could you keep it from me, for all these years? How could you keep it secret, and how could you keep it here?'

'It was dark under the table,' Russell explained calmly, 'and why would you look? Nobody was going to move the raft. It was too precious.'

As he talked, Russell prepared the

demonstration: he opened the small hatch on the surface of the box and then produced from his pocket something that Rose instantly recognized.

'My crystal!' Rose cried.

'No, Rose, it's another one,' Russell explained. 'There's still lots of cobalt, if you look in the old mine. And it needs cobalt. That's the thing, the whole thing, the data on Rixon's laptop showed me; it's like an instruction manual. That's why our parents came here, to source the special cobalt from Splinter Island. Without it, the battery is just a bunch of metal, wires, and superconductors. You see, you just need to do this.'

Russell placed the blue crystal inside the cavity beneath the open hatch. There were attachments to tighten: tiny screws which trapped the cobalt in place. Then Russell closed the lid. He pressed a switch alongside it. The reaction was instant. The battery hummed in a low drone, audible but gentle. Then came the lights. The first flickered green, on and off like the charging symbol of a phone with a loose connection. But it steadied. Then the second light came on, this time with a steady glow.

'What is it doing?' Rose whispered.

'Powering up,' Russell answered. 'It's getting ready.'

'For what?' Thorn scoffed. 'It just sits there. Will it make toast?'

Russell ignored him. 'Faith, can you reach it?' he said. 'I think you're tall enough.' He was signalling upwards towards the ceiling. 'Silvester fitted it,' Russell continued. 'It was supposed to run off batteries, but it never worked.' He was pointing to a dusty, cobwebbed lightbulb that hung uselessly above them, so dark itself it almost merged into the gloom of the ceiling.

Faith, her left arm at full extension, unscrewed the bulb and then handed it to Russell. He'd placed Cell Inverter 7 on the ground and now lowered the lightbulb towards one of the sockets at the far end of the box. Rixon didn't think it would fit, as the circular base of the lightbulb was the wrong shape. But it didn't matter.

The bulb lit up. Russell held it so it just brushed the surface of the battery, barely even touching it.

'Wow . . .' Rose whispered.

It was incredible—Rixon could barely believe it himself but the bulb seemed to be glowing brighter and brighter.

'Oww!' Russell suddenly screeched, dropping

the bulb to the ground. 'Too hot!'

But even as it lay on the ground, the bulb's brightness grew. A relentless energy pulsed through it.

'Get back!' Rixon just had time to yell.

When the bulb exploded, it threw a shower of glass shards into the air like a fountain of firework sparks. Rixon turned away, instinctively, but the glass still cut the back of his neck in pinpricks. He heard Rose scream and Thorn yell in alarm. But most of the shattered bulb landed on Russell. When Rixon turned to look he saw that Russell's blue baseball cap was almost white, covered in tiny pieces of glass.

Russell, however, didn't seem shocked. He was delighted. 'Well,' he said, shaking his head so the shards fell around him, 'it certainly works. I told you. That was the lowest setting,' he added.

Faith was staring at Cell Inverter 7 as if it was a tarantula. 'This is powerful and dangerous,' she declared. 'It should not be here.'

She was scared of it. Perhaps she was right, Rixon thought. Perhaps they should all fear what it could do.

'Russell, Rose, you must both go the store,' Faith decreed. 'There's a spade there. I want you to bury this thing, deep in the ground in the middle of the island . . .'

'But Faith,' Russell protested.

'Don't you understand? We must hide it. We must hide it until I decide what to do next.'

There were no more arguments. Rixon didn't want Cell Inverter 7 to disappear; he was only just beginning to imagine what it could do, but he was worried about Faith. He could see that burning look again and this time Rixon identified what it was: jealousy.

As soon as Russell and Rose had gone, Faith linked arms with Thorn. 'We all heard what Silvester said, didn't we?'

Rixon looked at her blankly, trying to recall which bit of the video Faith might be referring to.

'He said we must stick together, the Splinter Islanders, us.' Thorn nodded vigorously in agreement alongside her. 'It's like Thorn said, before; Silvester made the rules for us, he did everything for us. He didn't do it for you.' She was looking directly at Rixon now, Thorn was nodding again.

'Wait a minute, Faith,' Rixon objected. 'You heard him say that he'd left the island to me.'

Silvester said you should welcome me!'

But Rixon knew his allies Rose and Russell had gone, sent away on their errand. Faith had chosen her moment to reassert her power.

'The battery changes everything,' Faith insisted. 'We are in danger and you, Rixon, you make it more dangerous.'

'What?'

'Silvester said we must stick together. But you are an outsider. You could be a spy.'

'Yes,' Thorn growled. 'I said that, didn't I? I said that.'

'Faith, of course I'm not—' Rixon tried to speak.

'You're here for five minutes and then that man comes in his helicopter, from the government,' she continued.

'Trying to riddle us,' Thorn confirmed.

'So I have decided,' Faith said, 'that you will go home, Rixon.'

Rixon felt relieved. 'Of course I'll go home, Faith, if that's what all of you want. But we need to sort things out first. I mean, we need to make a plan, for when my dad comes back.'

'No, Rixon,' Faith said. 'You will go home now.'

'What do you mean?' Rixon replied, assuming she was joking, 'Even if I wanted to, how do you think I'm going to do it?'

'In a boat.'

'Oh, right,' Rixon replied. 'Well, I had a perfectly good boat, didn't I? Until someone decided to destroy it!' he said bitterly, pointing at Thorn.

For a second, Thorn looked sheepish. But Faith was unmoved. She spoke with complete conviction, like a judge passing a sentence.

'Rixon, we have a boat for you. It is ready and waiting for you right now. It is right beside you.'

Rixon suddenly felt as though the air had been vacuumed from his lungs. He was following Faith's glance. She was looking directly at the dishevelled, half-inflated piece of plastic on the table. She was looking at the raft.

Chapter 13

Power, Rixon thought to himself, that's what this is all about. Not the power in the battery but power on the island. Surely Faith now believed that Silvester was gone forever. And without him, who was going to run Splinter Island? Not the boy from the mainland, not the stranger. Silvester's video had made it clear that Rixon was the chosen inheritor of the island. It had therefore made it obvious to Faith that he was a threat. Thorn, of course, had always seen him that way.

So that's why they were standing on the shore, staring at the raft.

Thorn and Faith had needed all their strength to drag it from the museum to the sea. Rixon had watched with increasing distress as the plastic surface first became caught on a thorn bush and then snagged on a drooping branch of a birch tree. Thorn had made an attempt to reinflate the raft by simply holding one of the valves to his mouth and blowing. His lungs may have been strong but it made little visible difference.

As it sat in the water, the raft now looked more pathetic than ever. It was more like a collapsed tent than a boat. But Rixon knew he would have to get in it. There were two reasons for this.

First, he firmly believed that the boat wouldn't actually take him anywhere; this reassured him. The lagoon around the island was encircled by the wall, and the raft couldn't go beyond it. Second, both Thorn and Faith were pointing their spears directly at his throat. There was only one direction they'd allow him to move—out to sea, so that's where he had to go.

But the raft was ridiculous.

When Rixon stepped on to it, the surface sagged immediately beneath his foot and then rose up all around so that the whole raft became a 'V' shape. He also heard something that worried him—a hissing noise which could only mean air was escaping somewhere.

'Here you go, Rixon. It fell off the museum roof ages ago,' Thorn shouted, hurling a small plank of wood into the sea alongside Rixon.

'It's a paddle!' Faith explained.

She was trying to sound resolute but Rixon noticed a trace of doubt in her voice. It was insane; even Faith must have realized that. The idea that this craft could survive on the open sea, even if he could get there, was ludicrous.

'Start paddling!' Thorn ordered. He was still pointing his spear. So Rixon tried. He made a genuine effort. But it was impossible.

Every time Rixon leaned forward and dipped the paddle into the sea, he would splash water back into his face and into the middle of the raft. Every minute, the raft was filling up. Every minute, it was losing air. Every minute, it was more hopeless.

Rixon was inching his way towards the great canvas curtains. His plan was to get as close as he could and then just let the raft sink. He could swim back to shore from there; it was only a hundred metres or so. Faith would have witnessed his efforts. She'd realize going out to sea was impossible; she wasn't stupid.

And Rixon could now hear something else from the beach—a voice of reason.

'Faith, what's going on? Why is Rixon there,

in that?' Rose had clearly completed the task of hiding the battery and was now on the beach. Her voice was loud enough to reach Rixon. She sounded confused and angry.

'Get off!' Rose shouted.

That made Rixon spin his head round. As he floated helplessly on the raft, what he saw on the beach filled him with a new dread. Thorn had grabbed his sister and was restraining her with his arms across her shoulders. Faith, meanwhile, was doing something even worse. She was holding something to her lips. Rixon realized, to his horror, that it was a whistle.

And he suddenly remembered what that meant.

'Faith, don't!' Rixon heard Rose scream before the air erupted in sound.

First came the high-pitched blast of the whistle, followed by the mind-blowing, ear-splitting, response from the seagulls. It was happening . . . it was happening again, right above Rixon's head!

His gaze turned upwards as a cloud of birds filled the sky. The noise they made was already becoming unbearable. Rixon cowered in the raft, dropping the paddle at his feet and covering his ears against the howl and screech of the gulls.

They were doing it. They were lining up on top of the wall. The most outrageous, thrilling, mystifying sight which had ever come before Rixon Webster's eyes was now repeating itself right in front of him, and he was powerless to stop it.

The bills of the seagulls lowered to rest and bite on the top of the huge, canvas curtains that concealed Splinter Island from the rest of the world.

Rixon spotted the gap. It opened up right in front of him as he floated in the wretched, wrecked raft. As it widened, slowly and surely, Rixon saw the grey sea emerge in front of him. The wall of canvas gradually disappeared to reveal the vast openness of the ocean. The huge, moaning, rolling waves were sucking him forwards.

Rixon felt a sickness rise through his body. It overwhelmed his instincts and numbed his limbs. He could hear a howl of triumph from Thorn on the shore behind him. He could hear the crash of the almighty sea in front of him.

Then Rixon saw something else.

A huge silver yacht, shaped like a pointed arrow, was heading straight towards him.

To Rixon's terrified eyes, the silver boat looked like a moving mountain, towering towards the sun and looming ever closer. As it cut through the sea, it shot huge spirals of water through the air in its wake. Rixon clung to the raft. It shuddered and sagged as the new waves created by the yacht spread. Staying afloat had been difficult. Now it became impossible. One big wave simply tossed the raft over. Rixon was overboard. He thrashed his limbs in the ice-cold ocean and reached out desperately.

He grabbed something. It was metal. It was solid.

It was, Rixon realized, one of the vertical poles which supported Splinter Island's enormous canvas curtain. He now held it with both hands as he watched the raft disappear beneath the waves. If he turned to his left, he could see the beach. If he turned his head right, he could see the huge silver yacht. It was still coming, and it was heading straight for him.

Faith had seen it too. She was now frantically blowing the whistle, trying to tell the birds to reverse their action, to close the curtains again. But the seagulls were confused. They'd been told to let Rixon's raft out, and they'd obeyed their instructions. Now they scattered and circled in the sky, neither opening the curtains further nor closing them. There was a gap, and the silver yacht was ploughing on, straight towards it.

'Swim, Rixon! Come back, come back!' Rose screamed from the island.

Rixon knew she was right; he knew what he had to do. It was a race. He had to get back to the shore before the huge boat entered the lagoon and crushed him in its path. The vibrations from its engines rattled through Rixon's body as he began his first, frantic strokes of front crawl. Rixon felt the shadow of the yacht creep over him, he felt the waves of its wake beneath him, and he did the one thing he knew you must never do in water. Rixon could not help it—he panicked.

He felt his chest tighten and his legs turn to concrete. He was not going to make it.

He would not have made it.

It took two people to swim out and save him; it took two pairs of arms to drag him to the beach.

When Rixon looked up, spluttering on the sand, he saw Rose standing over him. But what stunned him was that, standing alongside her, shaking the water from his long blond hair, was Thorn.

'It wasn't fair,' Thorn explained simply. 'I don't

like you, Rixon, but it wasn't fair; your raft against that thing . . .'

He lifted up his huge right arm and pointed towards the yacht.

The tip of the boat's hull now filled the gap which had been opened by the seagulls but the rest of the yacht seemed stuck, too vast to force its way through. The children, however, could see enough of it to be sure.

'It looks like . . . his . . .' Rose whispered.

'Yes,' Faith confirmed, 'it must be his boat— Angry Potato Man's.'

They stood and looked at the towering bow of the silver yacht in silent, frightened wonder. All of them except Russell. Rixon couldn't see him on the beach. But he had noticed something on the boat.

It was there, just below the deck, painted onto the hull. A black creature like a crocodile with its elongated tail circling above the body and back towards the head; a caiman.

'Stay exactly where you are!'

The words boomed over the island from a megaphone. A man was addressing them from the yacht. They could not see him, but he could see them.

'I have a dozen security operatives with me here, all highly trained in different forms of combat. I instruct you to stay still!'

Faith turned, and for the first time since she'd forced Rixon onto the raft, she looked at him. She didn't apologize but she was searching for something, Rixon could tell. She suddenly looked unsure, even weak.

But if she needed a friend, it wasn't going to be Rixon. Not after the raft, no way.

'You don't know what to do, do you?' Rixon said to her.

Faith turned from him and stared once more at the great, intruding yacht. 'Get as many spears as we can,' she said. 'We will stand here and face them.' Her words were brave but her voice was frail.

Thorn, however, didn't need any more encouragement. He strode forward into the lagoon in the direction of the bow that stretched five metres high. Thorn versus the yacht; David versus Goliath, Rixon thought. For all the scars he bore resulting from Thorn's recklessness, Rixon had to admire his nerve. But it was pointless. Nobody can punch their way through a yacht.

At that moment, a different idea was starting to form inside Rixon's brain. It was a crazy plan, too wild to even put into words. It would depend on everything working the way Rixon thought it might, but there was no guarantee . . .

'Here, take this.' Rose thrust a spear into Rixon's hand. Her eyes were scared but she was ready. Her copper hair was tied back from her face and she held a spear in her own right hand while five more lay by her feet.

'We will frighten them,' Faith insisted. 'Then I will negotiate . . .' Her voice trailed away. Whatever scheme Faith may have been concocting, the yacht had another one; with a deep growl, its engines re-engaged. It was moving forwards, towards them, and nothing would restrain it.

A huge crack rang out over the island as if a mighty oak tree had snapped in two. The steel frame which supported Splinter Island's wall was bending and breaking. The enormous canvas curtain itself was now being ripped apart. The yacht was tearing down the structure that had kept the island secret for so long.

As the boat advanced, its main deck appeared, looming high above them. That's when Rixon saw him. He recognized him. The man leaning on the railings, looking down at the beach of the island; Rixon knew who it was.

It was the same man who appeared on the merchandising for every Caiman product; the same bald head whose welcoming grin featured in every Caiman advert. It was the face that had beamed towards Rixon when he'd breathlessly opened the packaging of his own laptop.

But what was he doing here?

Rixon had no time to work it out. There was no time for anything. The entire length of the yacht was now squeezed inside the lagoon. Rixon heard its hull scrape the bottom of the seabed as the water became too shallow. The tip of its bow loomed so close, Rixon could feel the spray fly up against his face.

'Run!' Rixon yelled.

'No!' Thorn shouted back at him.

Thorn's right arm was poised above his head, like the string of an archer's bow pulled taut and ready. Rose screamed at him to come, and even Faith was edging away from the shore.

'Run, now!' Rixon tried one more time.

Thorn didn't hear. Or he didn't care. He channelled every ounce of his body's strength into his shoulder. The wooden spear was propelled forwards in a spiralling arc. As it collided with the metal hull of the yacht, it chimed gently and then fell, harmlessly, into the sea with a pitiful splash.

Then came the response. The sickening rattle of gunfire.

From the deck of the yacht, they were aiming into the clouds above Splinter Island. It was a display of noise and power designed to terrify anyone who witnessed it.

This time, Rixon didn't need to yell *Run!*

The children were already sprinting for their lives.

Chapter 14

Rixon had never run as fast. Even though his clothes were soaking wet and heavy after the capsizing of the raft, he felt as though he flew through the forest. His mind was spinning. But he knew where he was going, and he knew the others were following him. They had no choice—there was only one plan now: Rixon's.

He stopped at the museum. Rixon knew the wind turbine was there, and he suspected Russell would be too.

He was right.

'Rixon, what's going on? I heard, I mean, I hid . . .' Russell was trembling at the doorway of the ramshackle shed.

'Where did you put it, Russell?' Rixon panted, bent over with his hands on his knees. 'The battery—please—tell me you didn't bury it? Not like Faith told you to?'

The other children were arriving now, gasping for breath. Russell spoke very softly.

'I couldn't Rixon, I couldn't damage it . . . all that soil and sand. Rose promised she wouldn't tell. I've kept Cell Inverter 7 here. I know Faith will be mad, but—'

'Russell, thank you,' Rixon interrupted. 'You've saved us. Just possibly . . .' Then Rixon turned to the others. 'Quick, we need to get the turbine!'

'What?' Faith protested. 'The turbine? Why do we need that?'

'Because it's powerful,' Rixon said. 'Because it's our only weapon.'

Thorn understood that, or at least he understood enough. He began scrabbling in the weeds where the propeller blades of the turbine had been hidden for years.

Still Faith waited, hands folded, head shaking.

'Faith, come on, you're the only one tall enough—grab it!' Rose implored her, gesturing towards the other end of the turbine which rested against the side of the museum. 'We have to trust Rixon now. Who else is there?'

Faith sighed heavily, but then she took hold of the turbine. With Rose and Rixon supporting the middle, and Thorn clutching the other end between the blades, they slowly lifted the four-metre metal pole.

Rixon was daring himself to believe his idea could actually work.

'Bring it,' he told Russell. 'Cell Inverter 7, and as many cables as you have—any which came in the suitcase, and any which came with the turbine . . .'

'Rixon, what are you talking about—?' Faith objected.

'Shush, no time, just carry, move.' These instructions came from Thorn. Rixon had never witnessed him giving Faith an order before, and, by the look on her face, it was an entirely new experience for Faith too.

The shock worked. They moved: back towards the beach, back into danger.

Rixon didn't know exactly what a 'security operative' was until he saw one. There were indeed a dozen of them on the beach. They were all dressed from head to toe in black—men with slicked-back hair and women with biceps that stretched their sleeves. They were wearing thick black belts with an attachment on the hip which Rixon strongly suspected to be a holster for a gun.

Splinter Island had truly been invaded. An occupying force filled the beach.

Rixon heard Thorn growl.

'Don't worry,' Rixon heard himself say although, even to him, the words sounded ridiculous.

'Rixon, there are too many. We must run and hide, right away,' Faith declared, lowering her end of the turbine onto the sand. There was only twenty metres of beach between them and the invaders.

'There's no point,' Rixon said. 'They will just find us.'

'What, then? What, Rixon? What do we do?' Rose pleaded.

'I know what they're here for,' Rixon replied, 'so I'm going to use it, against them.'

If Rixon was shocked by the operatives who stood facing them, he was even more surprised by his own calmness.

'Dig a hole in the sand and stand the turbine up in it, the best you can,' Rixon instructed. 'Then Russell, attach the battery.'

'No, Rixon, we must hide that!' Faith shouted.

Russell was carrying Cell Inverter 7 in his

hands and wearing a variety of cables around his neck like thin black scarves.

'Faith, this is our only hope,' Rixon said. 'Russell, you've got to attach the battery to the turbine. There must be a way of doing it.'

'I don't know; I've never tried,' Russell replied, anxiously inspecting the sockets on the battery. 'I need time.'

Rixon looked at the operatives on the beach and beyond them to the yacht and the bald-headed man leaning over the railings.

'I'll keep them away as long as I can,' Rixon promised. Then he slowly began to walk towards the sea.

'I'm coming,' Thorn said immediately.

'No, Thorn,' Rixon replied. 'You stay with Russell and the others, with the battery. They need your protection. I just need to talk.' Rixon looked at Faith, remembering the word she'd used earlier on. 'I need to negotiate.'

The man on the yacht, meanwhile, was coming to meet him, in an extraordinary fashion. Having thrown a rope over the railings, he was now abseiling down it. This, Rixon reasoned, was the way the 'security operatives' must have got down to the beach too. But they looked like athletes in the prime of physical fitness. The man coming to join them was twice their age, at least. He was wearing a cream-coloured suit and a red shirt. The same outfit, Rixon remembered, that he wore in all the advertisements for Caiman products.

'Whoah, made it!' the man shouted, releasing the rope and landing with a small splash in the sea. He waded the last few metres to the beach with a strange glow at the side of his mouth. Only when he came closer did Rixon realize it was the sun's reflection off a gold tooth.

'Horatio,' Rixon said aloud, suddenly remembering. 'Horatio Caiman; I knew it was a weird name.'

'Well, that's an interesting perspective,' the man replied, 'from somebody called Rixon.'

He made a signal to the operatives who simultaneously relaxed their stance and began to huddle together. They looked puzzled. 'Just kids,' Rixon overheard one of them say.

But if they were confused, so was Rixon. Horatio Caiman was world-famous. He'd built one of the biggest tech companies in the world. So how on earth did Horatio Caiman know who Rixon Webster was?

'Please, do not be alarmed,' Caiman said,

shaking the water from the bottom of his trouser legs. 'I should have worn shorts, I suppose, but this is a business meeting, after all.'

He flashed another grin and briefly scratched the top of his tanned bald head.

'Oh, sorry about your wall . . . thing,' he said, vaguely motioning behind him. 'We will repair it, perhaps. Such a primitive structure, but so effective! I can't tell you how many times I've toured this coastline, searching. I even used my private jet, to look from above, but all we saw was thousands of seagulls!'

He was now staring over Rixon's shoulder towards the top of the beach, towards the others who were—Rixon hoped—making rapid progress with the turbine.

'But surely,' Caiman said, suddenly frowning, 'those children . . . Don't tell me, they can't be—'

'Enough!' Rixon declared, loud enough to make a couple of the operatives jump to attention.

Rixon wasn't there to answer questions, he reminded himself. He was going to *ask* them.

'What are you doing here?' Rixon demanded, in the boldest voice he could summon up.

'Oh,' Horatio Caiman replied, spreading his arms wide, 'I'm just here to help.'

'Help?' Rixon spluttered. 'Do you normally bring a small army with you when you turn up to "help"?'

There was just a flicker of annoyance in Caiman's grin before he replied. 'Well, I always travel prepared. I didn't know exactly what I'd find, did I? Are there others? Here, I mean? It can't be just the children.' He motioned towards the top of the beach. 'What are they doing, by the way—building a windmill?'

Rixon ignored the question. 'You are trespassing on private land,' Rixon said sternly. 'You have fired guns and broken things and—'

'Calm, calm,' Caiman interrupted. 'I'm not here to hurt you. There is only one thing I want, Rixon, only one thing I've ever wanted.' He paused and the grin disappeared. When he spoke next, it was not a question; it was an instruction. 'Cell Inverter 7, tell me where it is.'

Rixon said nothing, trying desperately to make his face expressionless.

'Silence? OK, well, let me explain my story, and you can give me the happy ending. Deal?' Horatio Caiman cleared his throat and fixed his grin. 'In my business, information is everything,' he began. 'I will do anything, *anything*, to stay one step ahead of my rivals. So when some super-brain scientists were inventing a battery to revolutionize the world, of course I knew about it—I had to. Caiman Technologies will build the first aircraft to cross the Atlantic on battery power, Rixon; fact!'

He was sounding like one of his own adverts, Rixon thought.

'We had their lab watched, bugged, infiltrated,' Caiman continued, 'but they still got away. On a boat! On a simple, stupid boat. In the middle of the night.'

'Wait a minute,'—a sickening thought had just entered Rixon's head—'you didn't . . . I mean, the boat . . . did you put a bomb on it?'

Caiman stared at him, seeming genuinely perplexed. 'Bomb the boat? Rixon, why would I want to destroy them? I wanted the invention. I was willing to pay—anything!—but they never listened.' Caiman stopped for a second and scratched the same dry patch of skin on the top of his head. 'I never believed they were dead. I was convinced they were working somewhere secretly. I figured they'd set up a lab on a boat in the ocean, away from everything. That's why I scoured this bit of the sea.' Caiman turned to look back at what remained of the wall, the ripped sheets of canvas. 'But they were here, hidden? It's just too crazy . . .'

'No,' Rixon replied in a voice of cold stone, 'they never came here. They died on the way. Only the children survived.' He couldn't see the point of concealing it any more. The children of Splinter Island were there, in full view.

A grin spread across Caiman's lips, revealing the gold tooth. 'Well then, I must thank you, Rixon, for leading me here to them.'

'What? What do you mean? What are you talking about?'

'I told you we had the scientists under surveillance. Well, that means spyware, viruses, a whole war, waged with technology.'

'So . . . ?' Rixon could feel a creeping sensation like a spider crawling down his spine.

'So, guess what,' Caiman continued. 'The other day, completely out of the blue, up pops something in my data analyst's inbox. Something amazing! Somebody, somewhere has just opened up a file. A document all about Cell Inverter 7, infected with a beautiful piece of spyware . . .' Caiman paused for a second and smiled more sickeningly than ever. 'I couldn't read the document, Rixon, but I could tell exactly where it had been opened. And how wonderful that you use a Caiman laptop! Your Caiman ID made it so easy to find you, Rixon. Within twenty minutes, I knew more about you than you know about yourself.'

Rixon felt his legs shake as the truth gripped him.

'So,' he mumbled, 'you tracked me?'

'Oh yes,' Caiman replied. 'Mind you, it was very frustrating. Your laptop seemed to be on an impenetrable rock in the middle of the sea! We had to go back and refuel yesterday. How wonderful that today those amazing birds opened up the curtains to reveal this place; what luck! What are they, drones in feathers? You'll have to tell me all about it. Once you've handed over Cell Inverter 7. It is here, Rixon, isn't it?'

'Rixon! It's ready . . . I think.'

It was Russell's voice, from the top of the beach. Rixon wished he sounded more confident but it would have to do. He knew his plan was absurd. But at that moment Rixon would have tried anything just to wipe the glinting smirk from Horatio Caiman's face.

He turned and ran back to the others. As soon as he threw himself down on the sand alongside

Russell, he yelled the instruction: 'Turn it on!'

The turbine now stood in the sand, stretching upwards to the height of a lamppost. It was designed to generate electricity. But Rixon wasn't interested in that. He wanted to generate wind. He needed a typhoon on Splinter Island beach.

The three blades at the top of the pole began to turn, creaking after so many years of inactivity. And then they stopped.

'Russell, come on! We need to make it work!' Rixon shouted.

'Rixon, it's not even designed to function this way, I can't . . .' Russell was hunched over Cell Inverter 7, trying to force a black cable from the turbine into a circular socket in the front of the box. Russell could make the connection but, as soon as he released it, the cable popped back out.

'Argh, it won't fit!' Russell cried out in frustration.

'Yes, it will fit.'

Thorn grabbed the battery. He held the box in his left hand and jammed in the cable with his right. Thorn grunted with the effort as the connection crunched into place. The effect was instantaneous. The blades of the turbine span . . . and kept on spinning, rotating with frightening speed.

'It's gone crazy!' Rose shouted, fighting to be heard over the roar of the turbine. Then the vibrations started.

'We've got to hang on to it!' Rixon yelled. 'It's going to fall!'

The turbine was shuddering and sliding in the sand.

Thorn put his shoulder against the pole; Faith did the same. They both held on desperately, trying to keep the thing upright.

The blades of the turbine moved so quickly they went beyond a blur. The super battery was sending its power back into the machinery. The turbine was making wind rather than harvesting energy from it. It had become their weapon, an air cannon. And it was aimed directly at Splinter Island's invaders.

It had taken Horatio Caiman roughly a minute to work out what was going on. Over the space of those sixty seconds, his mouth had gone from chuckling to hollering, ordering his operatives: 'Forward!'

They didn't stand a chance.

'Get them! Get the battery! Get up!' Horatio Caiman yelled manically.

But whenever the black-suited operatives got

anywhere near the turbine, they were blown backwards. The wind was picking up pebbles, twigs, and clouds of sand, flinging them into the faces of the intruders, who were retreating to the edge of the sea.

'Yes, Rixon! We're winning!' Thorn was still clinging on to the turbine was his right arm but his left hand made a fist of victory. His eyes gleamed wildly in Rixon's direction. Rixon smiled back at him, sharing something which had previously seemed impossible: respect.

Horatio Caiman's cream-coloured jacket, meanwhile, was billowing with air. The force of the wind was blowing him off his feet! Two of his guards had to grab hold of his shoulders and pull him down as he wailed in panic.

Rose cheered, Thorn roared. Faith may have smiled—Rixon couldn't be certain, but he didn't care anyway. Thorn was right; they were winning. Rixon felt like a field marshal defending his very own island, vanquishing the invaders.

Russell, however, was worried.

'Rixon, look!' he yelled from his position, crouched over Cell Inverter 7.

'I am looking,' Rixon shouted back. 'It's brilliant—they can't get near us!'

'No, Rixon, don't look at the beach; look at the blades!'

Rixon jerked his head upwards. The blades were still spinning but their motion seemed skewed. Instead of making a perfect circle, they were moving almost in a figure of eight.

Then Rixon saw something else, something worse. There was a crack. It looked like a thin strip of lightning starting right at the top of the turbine and slowly zigzagging down the tower.

'Watch out!' Rixon cried.

But there was nothing they could do.

The turbine was imploding under the strain of the intense energy provided by the super-battery.

The coupling which held the blades to the top of the tower gave way. With a scream of steel against steel, the mechanism burst free and spun wildly upwards.

The three blades, still attached to their central hub, rose, circled, and then began to descend.

'Oh, my—'

'It's—'

'Where—?'

As the children watched, the missile of rotating metal fell to the beach, thirty centimetres in front of Horatio Caiman's feet.

Nobody moved, nobody spoke. Even the sea seemed to freeze. Rixon could see the wreckage of his grand plan half-submerged in the sand in front of him. One vertical blade stood upwards, its tip pointing towards the sun. It was almost tall enough to hide Horatio Caiman. But Rixon heard his voice.

'Get . . . it . . . now!' Caiman howled.

But none of his operatives moved.

'What?' Rixon heard one of them say.

'You mean the kids?' another asked.

'I'm not here to attack kids, sir,' the tallest woman of the group declared, her black-sleeved arms folded across her chest.

'Idiots!' Caiman shouted. He strode forwards himself. 'The battery, of course. What else do you think was powering that murderous machine!'

Rixon assessed the situation. Behind him was one broken turbine and four shattered children—even Thorn looked exhausted. In front of him stood a dozen black-suited invaders and one billionaire businessman who looked more furious than any other human being Rixon had ever confronted.

The game, Rixon knew, was up.

Chapter 15

The sight of Russell silently handing over Cell Inverter 7 with his head bowed and his arms trembling brought tears to Rixon's eyes.

The only thing that made it worse was Faith's comment: 'I told you we should have hidden it.'

Thorn could not bear to watch. He turned his back and hurled pebbles towards the forest.

Only Rose seemed at ease. She didn't pay any attention when Horatio Caiman gleefully grabbed the super battery either. She was looking upwards, towards the clouds.

'It's a shame,' Caiman declared. 'I would have offered you a fortune for this,' he said, cradling Cell Inverter 7 like a newborn child, 'but you wanted to fight. And you lost.'

When Horatio Caiman began to laugh mockingly, Rixon covered his ears. He was trying so hard to block out the noise that it took him a few seconds to realize there was another sound.

Rose was calling, summoning. *Kerrrr-yow! Kerrrr-yow!*

Horatio Caiman and his operatives stared at Rose as if she was mad. But Rixon knew that she wasn't. He was just starting to understand what she was doing.

Kerrr-yow! Kerrrr-yow!

Rose's voice carried a fierce urgency as she cupped her hands around her mouth and tilted her head back. When the response came, Splinter Island's invaders were completely unprepared: Horatio Caiman's elite band of security operatives had not been trained to withstand a seagull attack.

Within ten seconds, there were a hundred birds, circling and massing above Splinter Island. Within a minute, there must have been a thousand; far too many for Rixon to count. But the gulls seemed uncertain, chattering nervously, squawking for reassurance.

Rose seemed anxious too. She was still looking upwards and continuing to make her own squeals and cries.

'What's going on?' Horatio Caiman demanded. 'Is she controlling them? They're drones, aren't they? What's the trick?'

Nobody answered him. Rixon was scanning the sky, looking for the same thing as the gulls, the same thing as Rose.

'Danny!' she suddenly shouted, joyfully.

The leader of the gulls seemed even bigger than Rixon remembered. His dark brown wings spread so wide that, from a distance, he looked like a fighter plane. He swooped towards the beach so quickly most of the operatives ducked and fell to avoid him.

Danny looped round to Rose, giving her a series of quick, determined calls like a sequence of questions.

In response, Rose just pointed . . . at Cell Inverter 7.

Danny needed altitude to maximise his impact but he reached the height of a skyscraper within seconds. Then he pinned back his wings and dropped like an arrow. There was no time for Horatio Caiman to run, nowhere to hide. Rixon just heard him scream in pain.

The tanned surface of Caiman's head now ran red with a stream of blood. Danny's beak had found a target. But it was the wrong target. Within seconds, he was climbing again, and now the operatives knew what was coming.

They quickly formed a protective circle around their boss as he clutched the battery in his left hand, trying to stem the blood flow from his scalp with the right.

'Get that bird! You're supposed to be protecting me!' Horatio Caiman yelled.

Rixon froze when he saw how the operatives responded. All of them reached towards the attachments on their belts. As Rixon feared, these did indeed contain guns.

The first shots were not fired at anything specific but towards the sky in general. Danny had just turned to descend again and immediately activated an emergency stop with his wings, banking to the left and circling upwards once more.

Now Danny's own security guards came into action. The gulls had seen and heard what was happening and, as Rixon watched, displayed breathtaking bravery. Hundreds of birds simultaneously swooped towards the beach, protecting their leader, moving directly into the line of fire.

'No!' Rose screamed, before letting out a series of desperate shrieks and screeches.

If the gulls understood, they showed no signs

of recognition. They flew on towards the danger. Several tumbled to their death.

The operatives could barely miss, there were so many gulls to aim at. But while they were aiming upwards, they were not looking sideways, and that was to Thorn's advantage. He hurled himself into the nearest operative sending her, in turn, crashing into the man behind her. Thorn was like a bowling ball making the pins fly. Four of the black-suited invaders were on the ground when he finally came to a stop. Everyone's attention was diverted to him.

Nobody was looking at Danny.

The gull had a second to execute his manoeuvre and he did it perfectly, approaching so low that his wings almost grazed the sand. His beak was narrow enough at its tip to just grasp the hinge on the top of the battery, and his immense strength was enough to carry Cell Inverter 7 away.

Horatio Caiman stood in shock, his arm outstretched and suddenly empty. By the time he'd registered Danny's escape, and howled at his operatives to fire, it was too late. Danny was a brown speck in the sky, the metal box he carried glinting when it caught the sun's rays.

The world's most precious invention was in the possession of the world's biggest seagull. Horatio Caiman sank to his knees in despair.

Rixon was still looking upwards. The sky above Splinter Island was now clear, the other seagulls had dispersed.

'Where's Danny gone?' Rixon asked Rose.

'I just told him to get it,' Rose said, her voice little more than a whisper. 'I don't know where he's gone, though . . .'

She turned then and looked at the beach. At the sight of the fallen gulls, her eyes filled with tears. For Rose, Rixon knew, it was as though her friends had died. He reached out to her, but Thorn was already there, holding his sister to him with his right arm as his left hung awkwardly by his side.

'Are you hurt?' Rixon asked.

'Do you have bones in your shoulder?' Thorn replied, half turning to face Rixon.

'Erm, your shoulder is a bone, I think.'

'Oh, well, I think mine is broken,' Thorn concluded.

That was the end of the matter as far as Thorn was concerned, and Rixon had no further medical expertise to offer. In any case, further conversation quickly became impossible. The noise was too loud.

'There's more of them, this time!' Faith shouted, her voice just audible over the roar of engines and propellers.

She was right—when Rixon looked up, he saw four helicopters flying in a diamond formation directly towards Splinter Island.

He recognized one of them. The other helicopters looked different, but the security operatives knew what they were.

'Police!' one of them shouted. The effect was immediate. Whatever loyalty the operatives may have had towards their paymaster, they definitely did not want to be caught, armed, trespassing on a strange island occupied by a group of mysterious children. They all turned and began running towards the yacht.

'Come back!' Horatio Caiman called after them. He stumbled to his feet, tripped on a stone, and fell face down in the sand. When he hauled himself upright again, his face was streaked with blood and sand, and his jacket was ripped; his humiliation was complete.

The last image Rixon had of Horatio Caiman was his clenched fist waving helplessly in the air as his crew pulled him back up to the bridge deck of the yacht. The man who had abseiled down with an air of complete command was being roped back upwards in failure.

As he watched the yacht leave and the helicopters circle above, Rixon felt a surge of triumph. They'd won the battle of Splinter Island! Yes, he reflected, that might be true. . . but they had lost Cell Inverter 7.

Chapter 16

In the sky above Splinter Island, the helicopters faced a dilemma. They hovered indecisively for a while before separating. Two of the helicopters veered off in pursuit of the yacht; the others began their descent towards Splinter Island. The children were all gathered together on the beach, watching.

'One bully leaves, another arrives,' Faith said. 'That is your father coming back, isn't it, Rixon?'

'Yes, I think so,' Rixon replied. 'I'm sure he's brought food,' he added hopefully.

Faith sighed deeply and turned to face him. 'Rixon, we have lived on this island for years, in perfect peace. Then one day you arrive and suddenly, bang!'—Faith clapped her hands together like cymbals—'Everything has changed, everything has gone wrong. Now there is only trouble on this island.'

Rixon felt himself seething. The injustice of Faith's words raged inside him. Wasn't it his plan that had seen off Horatio Caiman? It was clear: the more he succeeded, the more Faith suspected him.

'Look, look at that!' Rixon began, throwing his arms towards the gaping space in the wall where the canvas had been ripped open by Caiman's yacht. 'That's the world there, the outside world, the real world! I know Silvester tried his best. I know he wanted to protect you. But you can't hide from it any more. The world is happening, and you're part of it!'

Rixon turned to see if there was any reaction from the children. Russell's blue baseball cap nodded, just once but with conviction. Rose's copper hair swirled around her face as she forced a look of determination into her eyes. Thorn, meanwhile, couldn't decide; he was turning his head between Rixon and Faith.

Faith stood, arms folded, shoulders back, a towering presence—still, in her own mind, the appointed leader of Splinter Island.

'Someone had to come,' Rixon continued, 'someone had to save you, someone had to bring you back to the world. And the point is, as you all know, as you *all* know—' he paused to fix his eyes on Faith '—Silvester chose me.'

Whatever words Faith wanted to throw back at Rixon, they remained unspoken. The whirlwind from the rotating blades of the two helicopters above was almost as intense as the storm generated by the turbine. The children had to run for cover.

But Rixon wasn't hiding. There was to be no more of that. As soon as the helicopters landed, as soon as the blades stilled, he marched forward to meet his father.

David Webster had threatened to bring the full force of the law to Splinter Island. In reality this amounted to three very young, nervous police officers, a spaniel, and two pilots, one of whom was holding a huge bag of miniature chocolates.

'Billy!' Rose shouted.

'Get your laughing gear around these!' he called back, hurling it through the air towards the children.

Rose caught the gift; Thorn ignored it. He prowled around like a wounded animal. Using his right hand, he drew a line in the sand with the tip of his spear and told the police officers not to take a step beyond it.

'Best listen to him, constables,' Billy advised.

Rixon, meanwhile, was waiting for his dad. David Webster was finishing a conversation on his huge, black satphone. He clipped it into his belt and marched across.

'What on earth has been going on, Rixon?' he demanded. 'That was Horatio Caiman, in the yacht, you know? Horatio Caiman!'

'Yes, Dad, I know.'

'We are tailing him. I've just checked, the navy will cut him off before he can get anywhere. But Rixon, you must tell me—it's absolutely vital that I know now—has he got it?'

Rixon just shook his head. 'No, Dad,' he said calmly.

'Well, thank goodness for that,' his father grinned in relief. 'So you can just give me Cell Inverter 7 and we can stop this nonsense. There's incredible interest in it. I've been talking to the highest powers, Rixon, and I mean the highest.'

Rixon noticed something immediately. His dad had not shown the slightest concern for the welfare of the children on the island. He hadn't even asked how Rixon was. All he was bothered about was the invention and his own plans. It was, in every sense, all about power.

So Rixon said the two little words again: 'No, Dad.'

David Webster gritted his teeth. 'Look, Rixon, this is serious. If you've hidden Cell Inverter 7 somewhere on this island, we'll find it easily. So stop wasting time and just tell me where it is.'

'No, dad,' Rixon repeated. 'What I mean is, I can't give you Cell Inverter 7 because I don't know where it is.'

His dad looked at Rixon as though he was trying to translate a phrase he'd heard in a foreign language. 'What on earth do you mean?'

'I mean that a bird flew away with it. Danny, the leader of the seagulls—he took it. We don't know where he's gone.'

It took David Webster three seconds before he erupted into laughter. 'Oh, Rixon,' he eventually managed to say, 'you and your stories. I remember that hilarious one you wrote, you know . . . When was it—at school?'

Rixon didn't remember and, more to the point, he knew his dad didn't either.

'It's not a story,' Rixon replied in a stony voice.

The others were near enough to join the conversation.

'It's the truth,' Rose confirmed 'Danny's got it.'

'He's smarter than you,' Faith declared.

'He could be a hundred miles away by now,' Russell added.

He could have been, but he wasn't. In fact, at that moment, Danny, possibly believing that the situation had calmed with the yacht's departure, was circling directly above Splinter Island.

Rose's eyes gave him away. She couldn't help looking upwards as soon as she spotted those huge brown wings. Rixon followed her gaze and so did David Webster.

'My, oh my, is that it? Is that bird really carrying it?' Rixon's dad was speaking as if he could not comprehend what his eyes were seeing. That happened frequently on Splinter Island, Rixon knew.

Danny still had Cell Inverter 7 in his beak. But the weight of it was clearly taking its toll. His flight, normally so steady, looked laboured. He was way above them, almost as high as the helicopters had been, but Danny was having to flap his wings furiously to maintain his altitude.

'What's he doing? What's he going to do?' Rixon's dad asked furiously.

'Well, that's up to Rose,' Rixon replied.

Rixon was convinced that Danny was waiting for orders. Rose had it in her power to communicate, to give instructions. But she herself was unsure. She looked at Rixon, her eyes asking him. But he didn't know. Rixon could only shrug.

Rixon didn't know whether Danny would even respond to a call from Rose—none of them could be sure about that. It was obvious that Danny was tired; even a bird of his extraordinary strength would not be able to carry something as heavy as the battery for very long.

And, of course, Rixon didn't know exactly what message Rose hoped to convey as she tilted her head back and screeched, *Kerrrr-ra! Kerrrr-hay!*

But within a second, Danny had opened his beak to reply. They heard his call reach them on the breeze just before the splash from the ocean. Cell Inverter 7 had fallen and, far from the shore of Splinter Island, it could only now be sinking.

When the realization of what had just occurred fully unravelled in David Webster's brain, he wailed like a baby.

When Rixon began to unbutton the blue and white shirt he'd worn since Faith had given it to him, the others immediately reacted as one.

'You can't,' Rose implored him.

'It's too far; you'll never swim it,' Faith told him.

'How will you get past the wall?' Thorn asked.

Even his dad told him to stop. David Webster had come up with a radical solution. 'We'll get a submarine,' he said. 'We can still recover it!' he insisted.

But Rixon was not thinking of Cell Inverter 7, not any more. 'I'm not going anywhere,' he said.

'There's no point anyway,' Russell said glumly. 'It will be ruined now.'

'What?' David Webster exclaimed.

'Once the seawater has infiltrated the circuit-boards, the whole unit becomes redundant,' Russell explained. 'Even if you found the battery, I'm certain it would be ruined.'

Rixon's dad took a step backwards, reeling at this final blow. Then he covered his eyes with both of his hands and shook his head slowly.

'It's over,' he moaned. 'It's the end.'

'No,' Rixon replied. 'It's just the start.' He turned towards the other children, still bare-chested. 'Thorn, do you have a spear?'

Thorn looked surprised but enthused by Rixon's sudden change in behaviour. 'Of course,' he replied, handing over the spear he'd used to mark his territory from the police. 'Are you going throw it at your dad, Rixon? Do you need any help?'

But Rixon wasn't going to use the spear as a weapon, or at least not in the way that Thorn imagined. He stuck it in the ground and then carefully tied the sleeves of the shirt to it, turning the cuffs into knots. Then, when he was sure the shirt was secure, he grabbed the spear with both hands and held it triumphantly above his head

'Do you know what this is?' Rixon bellowed, trying to make his voice more forceful than it had ever been before.

Nobody answered. Rose looked at Rixon anxiously while Faith and Thorn wore expressions of utter bemusement.

'Is it a riddle?' Rixon heard Thorn whisper. But he held onto the spear. Rixon looked up towards the sun and saw the blue and white striped shirt billow in the breeze.

Russell finally understood. 'It's a flag,' he said. 'Is that what you've made, Rixon, a flag?'

'Yes, Russell, it's *your* flag,' Rixon replied, trying to stretch his arms still further to raise the spear yet higher. 'It's *our* flag. The flag of Splinter Island. The Independent Children's Republic of Splinter Island!'

This time, the first person to respond was Rixon's father. 'What on earth are you talking about?' he said.

But Russell knew. 'Don't you remember?' he said. 'Because of our position in the ocean, over twelve nautical miles from the mainland, we are in international waters.'

'Yes, right, but—' David Webster blustered.

'So we are an independent country,' Rixon continued, 'owned—according to the wishes of Silvester and confirmed by legal documents—by me.'

Suddenly Rixon's dad didn't know what to say. He didn't know where to look. He turned his eyes to Billy.

'I reckon the lad's got a point,' the pilot said.

As for the police; the young officers were busy grooming the grateful spaniel. Thorn had drawn a line and they had no intention of crossing it. They knew they could enforce the law in their own land; but whose land were they currently standing on?

The citizens of the newly created republic, meanwhile, had flocked to their flag. They stood alongside Rixon. His arms were starting to ache but he did not want to lower that flag an inch.

'It's our country!' Faith proclaimed.

'With our rules!' Rose agreed.

'So all invaders must go!' Thorn continued.

Rixon briefly feared Thorn was talking about him. But the boy's eyes were fixed on David Webster.

Rixon's dad tried one last feeble attempt at laughter. 'Come on,' he said, 'you're not serious. I mean, you can't have a country run by a bunch of kids! You can talk about laws. Well, fine. Let me tell you this: no law in the world will allow children to live alone without a responsible adult!'

'I suppose that's me, then.'

There were reasons why none of the people on the island had seen the woman arrive. Most of them had been locked in the heated argument about their future, and, in any case, the woman had tried hard to remain unseen. She'd hidden herself behind one of the helicopters, watching and listening until she chose to reveal herself dramatically, at this point in the negotiations.

Now two of the people on the island recognized her immediately.

'Mum!' Rixon yelled.

'Oh, Rebecca . . .' David Webster mumbled.

Chapter 17

Rixon Webster was twelve years old and his world was a constant surprise. His mind was a revolving maze of secrets, sensations, and solutions. He had been thinking so fast for so long that when he saw his mum he collapsed.

That is to say, he fell into her arms, the flag dropping to the sand alongside them.

Rixon couldn't even remember the last time he'd hugged his mum. He'd never done it in public. But the relief he felt when she pulled him close in her soft, woollen cardigan was overwhelming.

'I should slap you, Rixon,' she said, between tearful kisses aimed at his cheek, 'only I think I'd like to slap your father first.' Rebecca Webster gently pulled herself away from her son. 'You have an almighty, humongous apology to make, Rixon. But I will hear my ex-husband's first.'

Rebecca Webster glared towards Rixon's dad.

'Look, Rebecca,' he began, 'this is urgent, vital, government business . . .'

'You said you would collect me in your helicopter. You said you would pick me up from North Niblington beach. You said we would come here together.'

'I know, I know,' David Webster replied, 'but the plans changed at the last minute, and there was no space. I . . .' His words trailed away. 'Sorry,' David Webster finally muttered.

'Yes, and I'm sorry too, Mum, I really am,' Rixon said, following his cue. 'I was so desperate to get here, to try to find Splinter Island. I never should have . . . done it, you know, like I did . . .'

'Rixon,' Rebecca Webster replied sternly, 'you shouldn't just be apologizing to me. You should be saying sorry to *him*!'

She pointed behind her, towards a ginger-bearded man forlornly trudging over the beach, the waves lapping over his boots. He was shielding his eyes with an enormous hand and anxiously scanning the shoreline.

Rixon's stomach turned a somersault. He'd never really wanted to see Asa Hartley again.

Now, Asa Hartley had spotted him. 'Aha!' he

cried, and began marching over.

Before Rixon had a chance to decide how he would possibly begin his apology, Asa Hartley flung him a question. 'Where is she?' he bellowed. 'My boat, which you stole. I've looked right around this place. There's no sign of her.'

Rixon opened his mouth but no words came.

'Rixon, answer Mr Hartley,' his mum instructed. 'We had to borrow Asa's brother's boat to get here.'

'*The Bonny Lass*—she's a cracker. Moored her up over there,' Asa Hartley explained, motioning with his head. 'We can just tie the ferry to her and pull her home.'

'Yes,' Rebecca Webster said, 'so could you please tell Mr Hartley where his ferry is?'

Rixon gave a big sigh and then simply said, 'It sank.' He cast a quick glance towards Thorn who almost looked apologetic in return.

'Sank?' Rebecca Webster said, incredulous. 'Mr Hartley's boat sank?'

'Well, yes,' Rixon replied, remembering Thorn's violent sabotage of the North Niblington Ferry. 'Just out there,' and he motioned towards the lagoon in front of them.

'And there is no chance of recovering her?'

Asa Hartley said in an ice-cold voice.

Rixon just shook his head and turned remorsefully to look at the sand.

'Well, thank goodness for that,' Asa Hartley declared. 'I can make a claim on the insurance.'

Rixon was baffled: Asa Hartley seemed overjoyed.

'Well, OK,' Rixon muttered.

'I can only thank you, really,' Asa Hartley said. 'She was insured for ten thousand. I can use the money to do something better with my life.' And then, improbably, he walked off, smiling.

Rixon could still barely believe that the problem had been solved so simply, when the next monumental one presented itself.

'So then, Rixon, what are we going to do now?'

That was the question his mum asked and the question Rixon didn't know how to answer. He just looked at the children. They were huddled together on the beach, listening and waiting.

Rose had planted the spear back in the sand so the flag blew in the breeze. Faith was still trying to stand tall with her arms folded at the front of the group. Thorn was trying to pretend he wasn't in agony, scowling towards the police officers but clutching his injured shoulder.

Russell, meanwhile, was almost hidden behind the others. He'd pulled his cap as low as it would go over his glasses.

'Mum, you can see them. They've got nothing,' Rixon said simply. 'And nobody else but me.'

'I thought you said they had their own country?' his mum replied. 'The Children's Republic of Splinter Island, didn't you call it?'

'Well, yes,' Rixon replied, trying to revive the courage and certainty he'd felt, holding that flag aloft, 'but, I mean, do you think that sounds crazy?'

'Of course it's crazy,' Rixon's dad interrupted.

'Actually,' his mum declared, clearing her throat, 'I think it sounds extremely exciting.'

Both Rixon and his dad then stared at Rebecca Webster in amazement. But, while Rixon's face opened into a huge smile, David Webster just looked furious.

'Rebecca, don't be ridiculous,' he thundered.

'Oh, so are you the only one who likes excitement?' she replied. 'You are allowed to fly off in helicopters, saving the universe, or whatever it is you think you've been doing, while I stay in little Gilberton?'

'Now, come on—'

'No, you listen, for once. This place, this

Splinter Island'—Rixon's mum extended both her arms as if she was ready to embrace the island and everything on it—'you know what it looks like to me? It looks like a blank canvas; it looks like a fresh start.'

Rixon could hardly believe what he was hearing. 'But mum, the children, everything . . .'

Gently, his mum took hold of Rixon's hand. 'Rixon, when I told you that I wished it was true, that I wished there actually were secret islands and new places where we could belong, well, I meant it. I just never believed it; you did. I wish I'd trusted you more. I wish I'd shared your faith. Now I need to know about the children. We need to fix so many things here, but I'm ready to try.'

Her eyes started to fill with tears, and so did Rixon's. He didn't care. It felt for the first time that, just possibly, everything could turn out OK. Then somebody shattered the illusion.

'Oh, how very romantic, how very poetic,' David Webster said. 'Forgive me for pointing out just one little thing—' now he swept his arm around in a grand gesture '—you have here a lump of land in the middle of the sea with no proper buildings, no electricity, no shops, no school. Splinter Island has nothing. So how, may

I ask, do you propose to get everything?'

Rixon's heart sank back towards his ankles. He had no answer to that.

But his mum did.

'Well, I will probably use the two and a half million which will be in my bank account within forty-eight hours,' she answered simply.

In the silent seconds that followed this statement, Rixon had never heard the waves lapping on the beach so clearly. He wondered, of course, if his mum was telling some sort of joke. But her eyes were deadly serious. David Webster's expression lay somewhere between contempt and confusion.

'What on earth are you talking about?' he eventually spluttered.

'My uncle, Silvester, the man who once owned this island, left his fortune to the North Niblington Society of Seagull Supporters—you remember, Rixon? It is some kind of group dedicated to the welfare of birds.'

Rixon nodded. Of course he remembered—it had been explained in the lawyer's office; they were supposed to build a floating gull hospital.

'Well, this morning, I got a phone call from that lawyer man—Arthur Cronk, is it?'

'Arnold Crump,' Rixon corrected her.

'Yes, that's him. Well, I only answered the phone because I thought it might be your dad. Of course, it wasn't—' she scowled at David Webster '—but I'm extremely relieved I did take the call. You see, it turns out that these seagull supporters were a *secret* society. And the problem with secret societies is that they are, well, secret . . .'

Rixon, still bewildered, nodded.

'Yes, so Mr Crump hasn't been able to actually locate a single member of this North Niblington Seagull Supporters brigade; there's absolutely no listing of them anywhere.'

Rixon's mind conjured up an image of them frantically constructing the curtain around Splinter Island, protecting—as they thought— the precious species of seagull which lived there, desperate to keep the whole thing secret and safe, to avoid any publicity or attention.

'So, what does that mean,' Rixon hesitantly asked his mum, 'about the money?'

'Well, old Crump says that I have, as the closest living relative, a choice,' Rebecca Webster explained, a glorious grin spreading across her lips. 'I can either hand it to the government or keep it. And you know what, Rixon? I think I will keep it. And I think I will spend it on the one thing Uncle Silvester dedicated his life to . . .'

'Splinter Island!' Rixon declared with a surge of sheer joy.

'Splinter Island,' his mum confirmed.

There was a lot to do in the next hour. The children of Splinter Island quickly grasped the key fact of the situation: for now, at least, they were going nowhere. Rixon's mum was an immediate hit. Faith, in particular, was warm and welcoming. This surprised Rixon at first, but then it occurred to him it was years since Faith had actually had any contact with a woman. Even the strongest, most determined survivor would surely miss her mother terribly.

Rose, with the help of the young police officers, conducted a kind of memorial service for the slain seagulls. Pebbles were laid on the sand alongside their burial plots and the children sang their anthem proudly.

Asa Hartley, meanwhile, had been preparing his brother's boat to make the voyage back to the mainland and seemed a little disappointed when Rixon's mum turned down his offer to travel back with him.

'Oh, well,' he said with a final wave, 'this time next week I will be on the other side of the world, or somewhere near it!'

Rixon wasn't sure if Asa Hartley planned to use the boat or an aeroplane, but he'd heard him talk about a 'new life' and Rixon wished him luck. He still felt bad about the ferry.

David Webster watched the whole thing with barely concealed disdain. His ugly black satphone had been ringing continually but he'd been ignoring it. He'd have to report back the failure of his mission to recover the most prized invention in the world at some point, but he was clearly delaying the inevitable. In the meantime, he still did his best to spoil the mood.

'So, it's happily ever after is it? You're all going to live here in some kind of paradise, are you? Well, can I point out that the lad with the hair and the muscles currently has a broken arm, and I don't see a hospital, do you?'

Thorn was, indeed, in pain. He'd been trying not to let it show, but he couldn't use his left arm for anything. As much Rixon hated to admit it, he knew his dad was right.

Until, once again, Billy stepped in.

'Let me take a look at it. I did my medic's training . . . twenty-three years ago. All pilots did, back then.' Billy smiled as he approached, and Thorn grudgingly allowed himself to be examined.

'Oh, it's his shoulder, and it's not broken,' Billy declared after some gentle prodding. 'But I'm afraid it's dislocated.'

'What does that mean?' Thorn inquired.

'It means it's come out of its joint, lad,' Billy explained.

'Oh, so put it back then,' Thorn replied simply.

Really they needed a hospital, a local anaesthetic, a specialist. Billy explained all these things.

'Well, if you don't do it then I will,' Faith told him.

'But you don't have any medical training,' Billy said.

'Exactly,' Faith replied, 'so, get on with it.'

'Yes, get on with it,' Thorn confirmed.

Rixon couldn't watch. He turned his head as he heard the crack and waited for the screams of pain.

'Oh, thanks,' was all Thorn said.

When Rixon turned to look, Thorn was swinging his arm 360 degrees like a gymnast preparing to grab the high bar.

'Did it not hurt you, son?' Billy asked him in astonishment.

'Well, it tickled a bit,' Thorn replied.

The last thing Billy did was fetch a picnic hamper from his helicopter. This was received ecstatically by the children, Rixon included. It was only when food arrived that he remembered how long it had been since he'd last eaten.

Dressed in a fresh shirt borrowed from Faith's collection, Rixon was so engrossed in a slice of cold pizza that he almost missed his dad skulking away. There was no warm farewell, no encouragement for the future. David Webster just muttered, 'Ridiculous, totally ridiculous,' and marched towards the waiting helicopter with the phone pressed up against his ear.

The police officers couldn't wait to get away, although the spaniel seemed keen to remain on firm ground, whining on the lead as they dragged it towards the cockpit of their helicopter.

It was only when both of the helicopters were out of sight that Russell approached Rixon and leaned in to whisper in his ear.

'It will take me a month, I think, maybe a little longer.'

Rixon frowned at him and swallowed the last fragment of pizza. 'A month? To do what?'

'To build a new one, of course,' Russell replied. 'A new Cell Inverter. I was thinking we could call it number 8.'

Russell's eyes were, as ever, impenetrable. But Rixon knew by now that everything Russell said was serious.

'But, how?' Rixon asked him.

'Well, I would need the equipment, of course, the highest-grade components. That won't be easy. And a lab, of some description, here on the island. We'd have to construct that. But we've got the main things, haven't we?'

'Have we?'

'Well, yes, Rixon, think about it. The cobalt is here on the island, isn't it? And so are the plans for the battery . . .'

'On my laptop, of course!' Rixon exclaimed, suddenly grasping Russell's logic. The computer, his most valued possession (manufactured by the hideous Horatio Caiman), was still in the museum.

'Russell, you're a genius,' Rixon declared.

'No,' he corrected him, 'my parents were the

geniuses. I just inherited the invention. I kept it alive, even if I couldn't save them.'

With that, Russell turned and solemnly walked back towards the centre of the island. He was retreating to his museum and to his memories, Rixon thought. All of the citizens of Splinter Island had experienced things in their life that no child should have witnessed. They were not children at all, really, Rixon reckoned. Their childhood had ended in that shipwreck.

But there was still so much they didn't know.

At that precise moment, they were laughing. Thorn was offering to demonstrate just how strong his left arm was by lifting Rixon's mum off the ground one-handed. She was declining the invitation as politely as possible. Faith, meanwhile, was urging them to save some of the food for the days ahead, appointing herself 'chief of chocolate rations'. Rose was promising to show Rixon's mum where they all slept. Rixon smiled to himself as he imagined her reaction to the floating caravan.

Without quite knowing why, he found himself walking to the edge of the beach. Rixon looked out at the wreckage of the island wall—the ridiculous, towering, amazing curtain of canvas, which had kept Splinter Island concealed.

Silvester meant well, Rixon was sure of that. But you cannot pretend that something doesn't exist when it does; you can't hide an island forever, and you can't hide people.

They had a chance now. A chance not just to exist but to honour Silvester's legacy, to complete the work of the scientists and, just maybe, to achieve something the entire world would come to respect and cherish.

As soon as Rixon began to imagine the future, a whole host of complications crowded his brain. How would they build what they needed here? How could he stay when there was school to attend, exams to pass, and qualifications to achieve? Gilberton wasn't far; it lay just across a stretch of grey ocean, but it felt a million miles away.

All Rixon knew for certain was that life had changed forever. He pulled his shoulders back, turned his eyes to the sky, and slowly raised his right hand to his forehead in a salute—to the future, to Silvester.

'We live free,' whispered Rixon Webster to the sea.

Acknowledgements

Thank you to those who saw the potential and then displayed the faith. Sincere thanks to my agent and to OUP for making this book possible. Most of all, though, my thanks go directly to my wife. No-one else displays such strength and such wisdom. And no man is an island, not this one.

Joe

About the author

JOE WILSON is a Sports Correspondent for BBC News and has spent over 20 years in various forms of journalism. He lives in eastern England with his wife and two children where he is part-owned by a half-poodle. This is his debut book.

Ready for more great stories? Try one of these ...

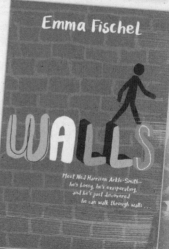